TRIGGER MAN

TRIGGER MAN

More Tales of the Motor City

Jim Ray Daniels

Michigan State University Press
East Lansing

⊛ The paper used in this publication meets the minimum requirements of ANSI/NISO
Z39.48-1992 (R 1997) (Permanence of Paper).

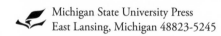 Michigan State University Press
East Lansing, Michigan 48823-5245

Printed and bound in the United States of America.

17 16 15 14 13 12 11   1 2 3 4 5 6 7 8 9 10

LIBRARY OF CONGRESS CATALOGING-IN-PUBLICATION DATA

Daniels, Jim, 1956-
    Trigger man : more tales of the motor city / Jim Ray Daniels.
        p. cm.
    ISBN 978-1-61186-018-4 (pbk. : alk. paper) 1. Detroit (Mich.)—Fiction. I. Title.

    PS3554.A5635T75 2011
    813'.54—dc22   2011008827

Cover design by David Drummond, Salamander Design, Inc.

Book design by Scribe, Inc. (www.scribenet.com)

green press INITIATIVE Michigan State University Press is a member of the Green Press Initiative and
is committed to developing and encouraging ecologically responsible publishing
practices. For more information about the Green Press Initiative and the use of recycled
paper in book publishing, please visit www.greenpressinitiative.org.

Visit Michigan State University Press on the World Wide Web at:
www.msupress.msu.edu

CONTENTS

CANDY NECKLACE

SHELLEY BIT ANOTHER HARD, TASTELESS BEAD OFF OF HER CANDY necklace. A yellow one. It tasted just like a green or red one. The flimsy elastic holding it together stretched across her mouth. Then, she bit off a red one—pink, really—and pulled the necklace back down over her neck. Sticky where other beads had gotten wet with spit.

Her mother, Ginger, sat next to her on the orange plastic waiting room bench in the emergency room at Mercy. Shelley pressed a huge bloody mess of towels against Ginger's arm as they waited to be called—so much blood dripping onto the floor Shelley thought maybe they'd have to cut the damn arm off, and then her mother could never hit her again, at least with her strong arm.

Candy had to look like itself to taste good, Shelley thought. Like candy bars. They were just bars. That was the perfect shape for chocolate. A rectangle you could wrap a hand around. Bite into. Candy that was supposed to look like something else always tasted bad: Candy cigarettes. Wax lips. Licorice shoelaces. Swedish fish—What made them Swedish? Did they swim with an accent? Sweden—what did she know about Sweden? Her brother, Randy, said they made porn there. He was seventeen and imagined pornography in his sleep. Shelley called him Porno Boy until their mother slapped her across the face. Randy had left home. No one had heard from Porno Boy in six months. Ginger told the school he dropped out, though he'd made no such official declaration on his way out the door. He'd stolen at least one car, apparently, so there was some interest in his whereabouts on the part of the authorities. Shelley's father, Stoney, was mad, because in his line of work, any attention from the authorities was not good for business. Stoney was a truck driver who delivered product.

Ginger—Gin, her friends called her, though Shelley didn't know how many people fessed up to being her friend these days—had an accident with a half-gallon bottle of whiskey. Ginger had let her drive to the hospital, though she was only fourteen. Her mother stretched across the seat and operated the pedals, groaning through Shelley's wide turns. *Gin Ginny, she wears her tight dress. Gin Ginny, her hand is a mess.* Shelley had never been in an emergency room before, though even she found that hard to believe.

"How come we're just sitting here? They should have a long sink for everybody to bleed in while they wait." Shelley chomped down hard and bit a few more beads off her necklace.

She was a smartass fourteen, which meant she was sixteen in certain states. She thought this might be an occasion to pull out her harmonica and wail some blues, but she thought wrong. Ginger couldn't hit her without taking pressure off her wound and risking another blood spurt, but she growled at Shelley so viciously that Shelley just blew one loud defiant note and put the harmonica away in the breast pocket of her shirt. The breast pocket—her breasts were a sore spot. Two sore spots—sore, and that was supposed to be a good sign. Something happening there that had already happened to ten or more of her best and worst friends, and it was time it happened to her.

"Don't you think it's time you stopped eating candy?" Ginger said.

"Since when is there an age limit on candy?" Shelley said.

Her mother hesitated—it looked like she was going to say something but then lost whatever it was in the fog of pain. Or, maybe she was just still drunk.

"You look like you're going to pass out," Shelley said evenly. She'd witnessed her mother pass out on numerous occasions, though never from loss of blood or shock or whatever her mother was experiencing at the moment that made her pale face wobble and sweat.

"What's it take to get attention around here? My mom's bleeding to death. What's it take to get some *stitches!*" She shouted the last part at the fat slouched nurse whose uniform buttons were pulling apart to reveal a lime-green bra beneath the white polyester.

Shelley would never wear a lime-green bra, she knew that much. Odd, lumpy vegetables. The green showed right through the uniform, like the nurse was some superhero with her costume on underneath. *If only*, Shelley thought. Then, her mother slumped in her seat and tumbled over, her head hitting the tile floor with a disconcerting clunk. At home they had wall-to-wall carpeting, her mother's drunken falls cushioned into incidental pauses in the angry static electricity of their daily lives. Lives in which Stoney made infrequent cameo appearances to either drop off some cash or hock some easily movable item, depending on the state of the nation.

"I saw a woman with two bras on today," her sister, Tina, said matter-of-factly. Tina could report on a gruesome car accident or the details of her bowel movements with the same voice—a reporter's voice, distant and authoritative. Tina was sixteen, and Shelley needed her to do more than report. Shelley worried that Tina was becoming an alien, or at least part of some other family—she didn't seem affected by the clichéd but intense drama of their daily lives: alcoholic mother, absent brother, absent father. Stoney was AWOL again, supposedly on a run to Florida to pick up some product. Tina and Shelley knew better than to ask about product. They took the cash when it was available and shut up about it. Stoney was a truck driver. That much was true, and they held onto that much.

"Two bras, huh?" Ginger said, a mouthful of tough chicken wedged into her cheek. "Maybe I should try that. For a new look. Maybe I'll get bigger tips. One for the price of two."

Shelley laughed. Tina laughed. Ginger laughed. But none of them were on the same page of laughter. None of them were in the same book. The dinner table had gotten stranger and stranger since Randy's disappearance and Stoney's extended wanderings. Most of the time, Tina seemed to be putting her mother on. Ginger was often so drunk, she didn't pick up on it, or, if she did, overreacted, overturning the table, lunging at Tina. It wasn't doing much for Shelley's appetite. For a while, she'd tried to put on weight, thinking that would help her figure develop, but she was thin and getting thinner. She was on a candy diet—lots of chocolate. Chocolate and cigarettes. She stole the candy from the drugstore at the corner, then bought her cigarettes there when she had the money. The clerks worked behind thick glass, and they weren't about to come out and try to bust someone for shoplifting candy. They put the cigarettes on the little bulletproof carousel, and Shelley put her money on it and twirled it around, and no one asked how old she was or why that candy bar was sticking out of her pocket. It was all part of the math of their gritty neighborhood. The old math, where you carried the one, and anything in parentheses was not big enough to be part of the equation.

"Two bras. One for each boob?" Shelley asked.

Her mother laughed so hard she sprayed pieces of chicken across the table. Tina didn't laugh. She should have at least smiled, but she didn't.

"No, one on top of the other. One was red and the other black."

"Hmmm," Ginger said. "Nice combo. I like it." She took a swig of wine from her jelly glass to regain her equilibrium, or to lose it again.

Shelley wanted to ask why someone would do that, but she didn't want to risk sounding like a child.

"She was standing in that tiny A1 Used Car office," Tina said. "The blinds were open. She didn't have a shirt on. Just two bras. A man was sitting at a desk watching her."

"Then what happened?" Shelley asked.

"I don't know. I guess she was putting a down payment on one of those junky cars in the lot. The light changed, and I walked home," Tina said.

The chicken was from the Colonel. Ginger worked part time at the Colonel's, a place where she did not get tipped. Shelley felt vaguely ill. The two empty chairs at the table were beginning to mess with *her* equilibrium.

"Mom, are you and Dad still married?" Shelley asked.

"Who told you that?"

"What?"

"That your father and I are divorced?"

Shelley gave Tina a look. Tina shook her head angrily.

"Somebody at school," Shelley mumbled.

Ginger took a long swallow, then poured herself another glass from the industrial-sized bottle she kept on the floor beside her chair like a cherished pet. She was taking too long to answer, so whatever she said, Shelley knew it'd be a lie. Ginger was not a good liar, though Shelley wished that she were just a little better at it. Sometimes she needed to believe a lie or two to get through a bad day.

"People shouldn't be spreading rumors like that," Ginger said. "Your father and I . . ." She closed her eyes for a long time. Shelley thought she might be on the verge of passing out, though it was too early in the day for that. She opened her eyes again, finally. "We don't have what you'd call a traditional marriage."

"No shit," Shelley said and instinctively ducked. Ginger just closed her eyes again, and this time her face fell to the side and into the open carton of mashed potatoes.

"This is happening way too often," Shelley said.

"It's becoming an unfortunate talent," Tina said. "A parlor trick, but we don't have a parlor. Pick her head up out of those potatoes, will ya?"

They looked at each other again, eye to eye. "My sources don't lie," Tina said. Shelley picked up her mother's head and rested it on one of those cheap Colonel napkins. "Pass me the chicken," Tina said. Shelley passed the bucket over.

After Ginger got her attention by clunking her head on the floor, the big nurse finally took her back behind one of the curtained examination areas. Shelley stepped outside and lit up a cigarette near a couple of young smokers in scrubs.

"Hey," one of them said to her. "Aren't you a little young for that?"

"Nah, this is a tough one," the other guy said. "Just look at her."

Shelley blinked through her thick mascara. "Fuck you guys."

"Whoa, and she's got a mouth on her too. What are you doing here? One of your friends OD? Or try to give herself an abortion?"

"C'mon, Gil, lighten up," the other guy said. "She's just a kid."

Shelley pulled down her tight top to cover her exposed belly.

"You guys aren't even doctors," she said.

The guy named Gil put out his cigarette and shook his head. "Kids aren't supposed to smoke. Stunts your growth." He stepped through the automatic doors and back into the hospital.

The other guy stayed. "We're nurses, actually," he said.

"My mother is getting stitches, actually," Shelley said. Cold outside, and she hadn't worn a jacket. Tina wasn't answering her phone. Shelley had school in the morning, and she didn't want to have to explain yet another missed day.

"Too bad. Is your dad in there with her?"

Shelley laughed. "My father is out on the road with a truck full of product."

The guy didn't say anything. He was squat and muscular, like someone who had wrestled in high school but was too short for football. His small movements on the concrete apron of the ER were graceful and fluid—confident. He had a tattoo on one forearm. Shelley couldn't tell what it was. She edged closer to him.

"I drove her here," she said proudly. "I'm hoping my sister shows up to drive us home."

"Your sister's old enough to drive?"

"Yeah. But she don't have a car. The car's here. What's your tattoo?"

"Can't you tell? It's Jesus and Gandhi. They're giving each other high fives."

Shelley'd been hoping the figures were in some band together. Some hip band she didn't know about. She took a step away from him. "I'd better go check on her," she said.

"If you need help, have them page me," he said. "I'm Mike Torres." He extended his hand.

"Shelley," she said and took his hand awkwardly. She rarely shook hands with anyone. She rarely touched anyone. Her cigarette had gone out. She quickly slipped it back in the pack and headed inside. She was shivering.

"I don't understand why you don't have boobs yet," Tina said. "You've got your period going and everything. Things should be changing."

"I think they're changing," Shelley said. They were getting dressed for school. "What are we going to do without Dad?"

"What we've been doing all along. How much is he ever here? And even when he is here, how much is he here?"

"I wish Mom was a little more here too."

"You can wish on that all you want," Tina said. Tina had a couple of hickies on her neck, Shelley noticed. She turned her back to Tina to put on her training bra. It was training nothing but air, but she'd insisted on getting a couple of bras just to be ready. Maybe if she put them both on at once. She laughed to herself and quickly pulled one of Tina's old T-shirts over her head. It was too small for her, but she liked things tight against her skin— nothing loose, nothing that could get caught, snagged.

"It's just me and you, Sis," Tina continued.

"Doesn't that mean we're fucked then?" Shelley said. Shoplifting and cigarettes. Cigarettes and swearing. Tina had been teaching her the fine points.

"Not necessarily," Tina said. "But probably."

Shelley wanted to hug Tina, but they didn't hug in their family. She wanted to embrace something solid. She wanted to hold onto the safety bar on the roller coaster and scream and scream. But Tina was out the door, so Shelley hurried behind her. Tina had a boy driving her to school some days, and some days he gave Shelley a ride too.

Ginger worked part time at two different restaurants. She had no benefits. Stoney's work did not come with any benefits written down anywhere. They were bogged down in antiseptic limbo. The ER had to take them, though the paperwork was immense. They wouldn't let Ginger go until she filled out a stack of forms about income and being uninsured. Shelley sat with her mother in a tiny cubicle as a man explained the forms and showed her where to sign.

Ginger was groggy and simply signed by the Xs. Shelley took their copies of the documents and looked them over quickly. She felt a flash of time spinning its wheels, doing donuts in a parking lot until it was facing the other direction and suddenly she was her mother's mother. It was almost tangible—a red buzz in her face. No way would they ever be able to dig themselves out of whatever debt they'd just committed to, Stoney or no Stoney. She shoved the papers into her purse.

"What can they do to us, eh?" Ginger laughed in an odd, forced way that led to a coughing fit.

The man behind the desk said nothing.

"Can we leave now, or are you going to lock me up?" Ginger asked.

"This is a hospital," the man said. "We don't lock anyone up."

Ginger's arm was wrapped in gauze and tape. Shelley didn't want to look at what was under there. She knew Ginger wouldn't be able to work for awhile.

On their way out, a doctor intercepted them, putting his hand up in front of Ginger in a preemptive gesture, as if to fend off a drunken tirade.

"Remember, you can't drive," the doctor said. Then, turning to Shelley, "She can't drive."

"We'll—we'll call a cab," Shelley said.

"Now, you remember, Mrs. Reed, what we talked about," the doctor said. "You've got this lovely young woman to take care of."

Ginger lowered her head. Shelley blushed with shame. The doctor turned quickly away from them.

They walked through the waiting room filled with the hurt and the scared and the angry. "What did you and that doctor talk about?" Shelley asked. "The weather? Sports? Politics?"

"Shut up," Ginger said. She sounded both defeated and smoldering with rage. "How the hell we going to pay for a cab?"

"I thought I'd drive home, since I did such a good job getting us here."

"I can drive one-handed better than you."

"Mom, your voice sounds like it's dipped in syrup or something. You sound worse—worse than usual." Shelley sighed. "I think they have a service we can use," she said vaguely. She rushed away to the receptionist before her mother could respond. "Please page Mike Torres," she said. She looked over at her mother, who had fallen back into one of the plastic chairs.

"Only doctors and nurses can ask for pages," the woman said.

"It's an emergency. This is an emergency room, right? He's a nurse. Just call and reverse the charges." Shelley felt a surge of power. Like she was holding the remote for the TV at last and would never let go.

"Is that your mother over there?" the woman asked.

Shelley waved to her mother, and her mother struggled to give her the finger with her undamaged hand.

"Did you ever think about what the fuck Mom and Dad were doing when they had Randy, you, and me, boom, boom, boom?" Shelley asked.

"I know one thing they *weren't* doing, and that's using birth control." Tina had become sexually active and had the pills to prove it, along with a purse full of colorful condoms that she seemed to spill onto the floor more frequently than necessary.

"Why did they want three kids? Why did they want to bring us into this? *This,*" she repeated, gesturing around the tiny kitchen littered with cigarette butts and empty bottles and dirty glasses, a room in which she could nearly touch all four walls from where she stood. Noon on a Saturday, and she and Tina were cleaning up from another one of their mother's small gatherings of like-minded individuals the night before. Ginger was in the shower, doing her own cleanup. Shelley had made earplugs from toilet paper and had wedged Tina's pillow against her head, but still she did not sleep until everyone had left. Tina had disappeared out the window for most of the night. Shelley had no idea when she'd returned to claim her pillow.

"They must have been in love," Tina said. "Or stoned out of their minds, which I think is kind of like the same thing."

"You may have been stoned before," Shelley said. "But you've never been in love. You've got all those balloons in your purse, but you don't love Eddie, do you?"

"When you get boobs, you come back and talk to me," Tina said.

"Come back. From where? We share a bed, remember?"

"They must've had health insurance back then. I hear having a baby costs a mint these days," Tina said.

Shelley found a rolled-up dollar bill on the floor, smoothed it out, folded it in half, and slipped it in her pocket.

"Don't let any drug-sniffing dogs get near that dollar," Tina said.

Shelley shrugged. She wiped her hands on her jeans.

"It'd be nice to have health insurance," Shelley said. "Maybe health insurance and a dog. Health insurance, a dog, and a backyard where we could grow sunflowers, and a vacation at the beach."

"You're losing it, sister," Tina said.

"All of us, the five of us in bathing suits laying in beach chairs in sunglasses under a big umbrella, and we have cold drinks."

"Cold drinks. That's part of the problem here, don't you think?"

Mike Torres appeared embarrassed when he saw Shelley sitting with her mother. He glanced at the receptionist and gave an exaggerated shrug.

"Hey, girl," he said to Shelley. "I assume this is your lovely mother."

Ginger gave him a foul look but said nothing. Her eyes drifted shut.

"What can I do for you?"

He seemed a little irked, but Shelley did not care. She had the papers in her purse. She had the keys in her purse.

"We need a ride. My sister didn't show. We can't—we don't have cab money." She smiled and tilted her head in what she thought might be a flirtatious way. She imagined it was what Tina might do.

Mike sighed. "Shit."

"C'mon, Mike Torres," Shelley said. "Be a man."

He raised an eyebrow at her. "How far you live?"

"Not *too* far," Shelley said. She stretched back so that her shirt pulled up above her navel.

"Give me fifteen minutes," he said and hurried off. He was true to his word, for a short while later he appeared with a stained brown leather jacket over his scrubs.

"I'll get my car. Meet me outside with the old lady."

Ginger was asleep, and Shelley roused her.

"Come on, Mom, you don't need crutches. You hurt your *hand*, remember?"

Mike's car smelled like pot and aftershave. It was spotless. A silver cross hung from the rearview mirror, along with some colored beads. When Shelley saw them, she reached up to her neck. She was still wearing the candy necklace. She quickly yanked it over her head and stuffed it in her purse, a large, black cloth bag that Tina called her bag of tricks. She often rested a hand inside it like it was a sling. Shelley sat in the front with Mike while

Ginger slumped down in the back, and they drove off from Mercy and into the city.

Shelley squirmed in the silence. She pulled her harmonica out of her purse and started playing the theme from the Flintstones. She'd had two lessons from a friend of Stoney's who played in a blues band in town and, like many musicians, seemed enamored of the product. She knew "Happy Birthday" and "Pop Goes the Weasel." Her goal was to be able to play "Whammer Jammer," but she hadn't gotten past Wham.

"You're just full of surprises," Mike said. "You know any songs about Jesus?"

"Yeah. I know 'Yabadaba Jesus,' listen."

She continued playing the Flintstones theme song. "From . . . town . . . Bedrock," Ginger mumbled groggily from the backseat.

"So, what's the deal with her?" Mike asked under his breath.

Shelley turned around and looked at Ginger. Her eyes were closed, again, delirious in Bedrock.

Shelley turned back to Mike. She realized that saying it aloud would make it true, but she knew it was more true than anything.

"She's an alcoholic, for starters," she said.

"So your dad's got a paper route on Mars, and your mom's a drunk. What's for finishers?"

"He delivers product," Shelley repeated. "They're getting divorced," she added, since apparently that was true too.

Ginger groaned from the backseat.

"And this sister of yours?"

"She's good," Shelley said, though she wasn't sure. She broke the elastic from the candy necklace with her sharp fingernails and then popped a few loose beads into her mouth.

"Turn here," Shelley said.

"And *this* is your street?"

Shelley hadn't thought much about where they lived. It was just home. They had a tiny two-bedroom house Stoney had paid cash for at a time when their lives resembled the normal lives Shelley saw on TV, except that no one ever paid cash for a house.

The street was littered with empty lots where houses had once stood, where no one would ever build again. To Shelley, the weedy lots were just part of the landscape, like someone who'd lost teeth through no fault of their own.

"You're getting me down, Mike Torres," she said. "This is the house, right here."

"I'm just saying—look, I forgot your name—I'm just saying, this is no picnic grove you're living in."

It hit her hard that he had not remembered her name. She put her hand on the door handle. "Shelley," she said. "My name is Shelley. You don't need to tell me about where I live." She had not cried in years, but she felt like she was going to. The car stopped, and she yanked up on the handle and jumped out, then reached into the backseat to help her mother.

Behind her, Mike Torres gently touched her shoulder. "Let me get her. I do this for a living." He lifted Ginger up, and she roused her head.

"Who the fuck are you?" she asked.

"Mike Torres," he said. "I'm a nurse who's helping you get back home." He opened his coat to reveal his blue scrubs.

Shelley envied the clarity of that statement. She wanted to say, "I am Shelley Reed. I'm someone who's doing something." Even if it was a lie. Even if it was only true for a few seconds.

Ginger seemed to accept Mike, taking his hand as he guided her to the door and inside while Shelley led the way, unlocking the door with her mother's key and holding it open for them.

Inside, the broken bottle and the trail of blood and the smell of whiskey hit her all at once. It made Shelley want to vomit, but she swallowed hard and quickly led Mike to Ginger's bedroom, where he eased her onto the unmade bed.

"Thank you, young man," Ginger said. She turned her head to the wall and closed her eyes again.

Shelley heard laughter coming from the room she shared with Tina. She slipped across the hall and cracked the door open. Tina was in their bed with Eddie, the guy who drove to school.

Tina looked up. "What the fuck, Shelley. Is Mom okay?"

"You got the message? Why didn't you come?"

Tina looked at Eddie. He laughed. Shelley slammed the door on them. Mike stood at the door, jangling his keys.

"Gotta run, girl," he said. She looked at him. "Shelley," he said and smiled.

Shelley suddenly pushed herself forward and into his arms, wrapping them around the leather jacket, squeezing hard as he tried to pull away, squeezing until he gave in and hugged her back.

"Don't go," she mumbled into the soft leather of his jacket.

"You gotta let me go," he said. "I'm sorry."

"Kiss me, Mike Torres," she said, brushing her cheek against his. "I'm going to be cleaning up whiskey and blood and glass as soon as you leave."

"Girl," he said. "Girl," he pushed away from her, hurried out the door, and drove away.

Shelley had heard the name Gandhi before but didn't really know who he was. If he was high-fiving Jesus, he must've been somebody important, though it looked like he was wearing a diaper in that tattoo. She didn't know a hell of a lot about Jesus either, except for Christmas and Easter—she was a little murky on what happened in between. At least Mike Torres had his heroes. Why couldn't he have been hers? Now he was back in his sweet-smelling car, driving away into the thick darkness that had taken her father and brother. She wanted it to take her too. She wanted to buy a ticket on darkness and let it take her on a long ride, but she had no currency recognized by night. She had a candy necklace.

Her shoe crunched against broken glass. The bright overhead light created garish sparkles off of the ruins. How could Tina just walk right past it? How could she get the phone message from the ER and not care? Shelley felt like she was exploding out of her skin. The two bedrooms were full, and the living room was a crime scene. She had nowhere to go in that tiny house that wasn't tainted.

She went into the bathroom and locked the door. She removed her tight shirt and her flimsy bra and stared at herself in the mirror above the sink. She applied more mascara and eyeliner until her eyes were black holes. She rouged her cheeks bright red, but she was still Shelley. She removed her jeans and underwear. Tina was pounding on the door now, and she heard her mother's muffled voice demanding something. She turned on the water to drown out their voices.

She pulled the hospital papers out of her purse and folded them into paper airplanes the way her father had taught her once, when he was home and she was a child. She creased each document hard against the bathroom tile, then cranked open the window. She lit each piece of paper with her lighter and sent them sailing out into the night to see how far they could travel before turning to ash.

TRIGGER MAN

THE WIND WHIPPED AROUND THE CORNER LIKE THE SUDDEN SWIPE of Curtis Lee's fist. At the party, Curtis had knocked Ronnie sprawling to the ground for being too drunk to get out of his way—reason enough for Curtis. Ronnie leaned his drunken self into the Funke Street wind. He was almost home.

The wind, the wild-west Motor City wind. Ronnie swayed, bellowing at the streetlight, the closest source of light in a black night sky crowded by factory smoke and its subtle stench. It burned his nostrils, carried up from the Rouge River in invisible boxcars, and what could he do but breathe it in as he—as they—always did. Him, Curtis, all of them.

Ronnie slipped on the icy street, and his head fell back against the curb. He lay sprawled there, watching a small spray of snowflakes drift through the streetlight's silent circle. He felt like that light—insubstantial, limited. He thought he just might fall asleep. He closed his eyes and rode the blue wave under his eyelids. He wanted to be sick, but it seemed like too much work. The cold was a vague menace, a pest, a teacher, a boss—it wanted something from him. Perhaps he could fall asleep and never wake up. He laughed at that. He hiccupped. His eyes closed again, weighted with the long night and everything wrong about it. Sleep—the tingle of it entered his bones.

A car swerved through the turn at the corner. Its misaligned headlights momentarily fooled the streetlight into dimming. It almost skidded over his legs extending into the road, then jerked to a stop. Ronnie felt his lips part into a crooked smear.

"Hey, buddy, need some help?"

Ronnie caught the spark of a cigarette through the rolled-down window of a dark blue sedan. "Are you my buddy?" he shouted.

"I wouldn't go that far," the man said. "But this don't look like the best place to be taking a snooze. You loaded? I'll take you home."

"Hmph," Ronnie said, drifting slowly back toward the lure of free fall. He forced one eye open. "You got a warmer in there? I need a warmer."

"A warmer? Yeah, I got heat. But I'm letting it all out of this fucking window, so if you want a ride, get your ass in here now or I'm gone. Just tell me your name so when I read it in the paper, I'll be able to say, 'Yeah, I tried to help that asshole, but he wanted to die.'"

Ronnie flipped over, lifted himself onto his hands and knees and promptly vomited onto the hard-packed snow.

"Hey, there you go," the man said. "You ain't gonna die—but you ain't getting in my car with that shit." He rolled up the window and fishtailed off down the street.

Ronnie wiped his mouth. He shook like a wet dog, then wobbled to his feet. He only lived a few houses from the corner. The man he had not recognized immediately was Alfonso's father. Divorced from Alfonso's mother, he still cruised by late at night to check up on his ex. The dark sedan's brake lights—he recognized the car now—flashed red at the other end of the block where Alfonso lived. It idled briefly, then sped off and out of sight.

"Fucking Alfonso," Ronnie slurred. The wind twisted him away from his house, but he turned back to face it, flush against his numb cheeks. He grimaced at the taste in his mouth. "Alfonso's old man. He ain't my buddy!"

He'd briefly hoped that it was one of his friends—Steve, or maybe Earl, cruising the streets after the party—maybe with Carol. Carol, concerned for his well-being after witnessing the quick ass-kicking. Lump on his forehead—he could feel that. And a lump in the back where he'd fallen. He was lumpy. He was bumpy. Ronnie'd been so drunk, Curtis had simply wandered away from him curled against the bricks on the side of—whose house was it? Some sophomore stupid enough to let word get out that his parents were out of town.

Hell, there isn't even any blood, Carol would've said if she'd found him lying there. *But I'm tender to the touch,* he'd explain, holding his groin. That's how it was with him and Carol. They'd grown up stealing each other's toys and plotting against their parents. She lived two doors down. She didn't care about him in that way—tender. While she'd be happy to kiss him, and maybe more if the mood struck her, him getting roughed up—well, she wouldn't lose sleep over that. She'd wanted to kick his ass plenty of times herself.

Ronnie slid down the icy sidewalk past Carol's house. Her old man was a lazy shit who never shoveled. She must've still been at the party. She'd talk to him the next day and give him the party recap and, incidentally, ask how he was. He slouched into the dark slit between houses and up to his side door. He yanked off his gloves, and they fell fingers-up into the snow. He laughed. Tender to the touch. His head hurt, and it'd hurt more tomorrow. He dug into a pocket of his tight jeans till he emerged with a key and a handful of loose change. The money disappeared into the dents it made in the snow, but he clutched the key, slipping it into the lock. He pushed the door open and swayed from wall to wall down the stairs of the dark house to the basement bedroom he shared with his brother, Ed. He fell face down on his bed and yanked a blanket up over his head.

"Hey, asshole, go close the fucking door," Ed hissed, then stomped up the stairs and closed it himself before angrily stomping back down. "Dipshit," he spat, then threw another blanket over Ronnie and fell back into his own bed.

A Lincoln Town Car. With that "contemporary elegance accented by an assertive road presence," Alfonso told him and Carol, as if reading from some slick brochure. Monday, and they were walking to school together, as usual. Ronnie'd told him about the encounter with his father. He'd already told Carol. He'd already asked her to touch his tender spots and got a laugh. A laugh from Carol was as good as a kiss.

17

"The point of this is?" Alfonso asked. "To show what a dumb fuck you are to be either run over or frozen to death five doors down from your own fucking house?"

Ronnie laughed, then punched Alfonso hard in the shoulder. Some people had glass jaws. Alfonso had a glass shoulder.

"Ow! Fuck off, man," Alfonso said, rubbing the spot like it was a stain. He was unhealthily thin, his ribs sunken in like some deadly disease was eating away at him. He dressed in all black and wore shit-kicker boots. Everybody knew he wasn't kicking any shit, but the rumors of his father's ties to the vegetable-market Mafia gave him a cushion, and people let him yap his yap. Ronnie and Alfonso and Carol had been walking together since grade school. Though they never hung out with him anymore—it didn't seem like anyone did. They were both sixteen, but Alfonso was seventeen, having flunked second grade because he still couldn't read. For awhile, he and Carol had tried to ditch Alfonso—to leave earlier or later to miss his morning arrival in front of their houses—but they'd felt a vague sense of disloyalty to the street. Alfonso was *their* asshole. It was a spell they didn't want to break. As if ditching Alfonso would mean ditching their entire childhoods.

A week later, Ronnie was walking home from another lame party—he had a license but no car—when he noticed the Town Car again, and Mr. Cardenal slumped over, asleep, the engine running, exhaust wafting up and into the cold midnight wind.

Their street was a funnel for wind, some odd geometrical or meteorological phenomena. One block over, you could light a match and watch it burn down to your fingers, but on Funke Street, it was nothing but blowhard ghosts booing the boring sameness of the box houses.

"Hey, Alfonso's dad," Ronnie said, tapping gently on the window with his gloved fist. "You okay?"

The man stirred. He rolled down his window and leaned toward Ronnie. Ronnie stepped back from the car. "Just checking, you know, and to thank you for offering me the ride last week."

"You're a wise man not to take a ride from me," Mr. Cardenal said, then paused. "So, you gonna kill her for me, or what?" he asked, as if they'd been in the middle of a conversation and Ronnie had been holding things up.

Ronnie screwed up his face.

"Why don't you get in the car and we'll talk about it."

"You just told me I was wise not to get in your car."

"This is true, my friend, but we are no longer discussing wisdom. We are discussing the potential employment of yourself."

"Kill who?"

"Get in the car. She's driving me crazy. You know whose car that is in the driveway?

"Looks like my Uncle Ray's Buick."

"Your Uncle Ray's fucking my wife?"

"I said it *looked like* his car. My Great-Uncle Ray is eighty-five years old. He ain't fucking nobody."

"Yeah, but he's still driving at eighty-five. Some guys, they hit eighty, they fall apart, start crapping themselves and calling their kids bird names and shit."

"Bird names and shit?"

"That's what my old man did. I was woodpecker, but he shortened it to pecker."

"You think maybe the name Cardenal—you know, cardinal—got him on the bird thing?"

"Some guy's fucking my wife who stole the car of an eighty-five-year-old man. How low is she gonna stoop?"

Ronnie shivered. He walked over to the passenger side and pulled open the thick door. "Contemporary elegance," he said.

"You should feel its assertive road presence," Mr. Cardenal said. He immediately pulled a large handgun from under his leather jacket and set it down on the seat between them.

"Been carrying the damn thing around so long, I can even sleep with it digging in my side. That's what that woman's done to me."

"Killing, that's serious shit," Ronnie said. "Why don't you do it? You've got the gun and everything right here."

"*You* are the 'and everything.' I can't do it, son. I still got it for her here." He punched his chest so hard Ronnie felt the vibration from the thump.

"Hey, are these seats heated?"

"Yeah, this thing's loaded."

Ronnie paused, then looked at the gun again. "Cool. Heated seats. If I knew you had heated seats, I would've taken that ride last weekend."

"You were one drunk motherfucker, my friend. You stay away from Alfonso with that shit."

That threw Ronnie off—Alfonso didn't seem like a part of all this. He was like a tacky lawn ornament or a Christmas decoration somebody'd forgotten to take down. Ronnie laughed. Mr. Cardenal gave him a hard look. "No drinking for Alfonso. . . . You know I ain't nothing but serious."

Ronnie nodded. Alfonso would break in half or his bones would melt if he drank too much, but Ronnie didn't want to point that out to his father.

They sat in silence for a long minute. The heat was burning through his jeans.

"Well, I gotta go. Sorry, but I can't kill your wife."

"Ah, that's okay, kid. It was just the insomnia talking."

"You were sleeping."

"So why'd you wake me up? Just so I can look at that fucking pussy car in my driveway?"

"I thought you might be dying—carbon monoxide."

"You think a Lincoln Town Car's gonna let any of that into the interior?" He laughed. "This thing's hermetically sealed."

"You know, your headlights turn off streetlights."

Mr. Cardenal pointed to his head. "I had them adjusted to do that. They turn off streetlights. They shine right in her windows. Just trying to mess with her head. Get inside her head. Her head and the head of the motherfucking old-man-car-stealing. . . ."

Ronnie started to open the door. "How much do you pay for killing somebody?"

Mr. Cardenal laughed, and his laugh turned into a cough. "What do I know—I'm just a numbers guy. This," he said, picking up the gun again, "this is just a prop."

"Can I hold it?" Ronnie asked.

Mr. Cardenal lifted his arm and checked his thick gold watch. "Nah, not tonight. Your uncle ain't coming out anytime soon. I'm going home."

Ronnie slammed the car door, and it made a solid thud like he imagined an airplane might make, or a spaceship. He waved to Mr. Cardenal, who eased his car into the icy ruts in the middle of the street. Ronnie felt cold-butt sad as he turned and walked toward home. It was three, maybe four in the morning. Darkness draped all of the windows in all of the houses.

After unlocking the side door, he gently shoved it closed behind him, giving it a little shoulder to lift it solid against the doorjamb, then sliding the chain lock into place. He took off his shit-kicker boots and tiptoed down the stairs. Ed had to get up for work soon. Twenty years old, he worked as a welder down at the Ford plant. He'd make a racket to wake Ronnie up. Ronnie'd have to pull a pillow over his head and wait it out, fall back asleep till noon. His mother had the tiny house's only bedroom. The little box heated up in the summer, and the basement became a refuge, but it was a house of cards, and in the winter the thin walls themselves seemed to shiver with cold.

He wondered how you could kill a person. A human being. To take away their breath and keep going yourself, moving forward, not looking back. Was it possible? Someone had killed his father. Was that person still alive?

"Curtis Lee is looking for you, Ronnie," Carol said. It was Sunday afternoon, the day after his latest encounter with Mr. Cardenal. They sat on the curb in front of the Porters, the one house between theirs. The Porters were an older, childless couple who had given them candy when they were children simply for coming to the door and chanting *Por-ter, Por-ter, Por-ter-er.* Their little dachshund, Pebbles, had died the previous summer, and they had invited the neighborhood kids over for a wake, but they were all teenagers and did not need or want the stale Tootsie Rolls. Ronnie and Carol thought it was pitiful how they dressed that dog up in sweaters and treated it like a human being when it was just a dog. They'd never been to a funeral before, and they agreed that they weren't starting with dogs.

The curb was neutral territory. Over the years, when Ronnie or Carol needed to talk, they'd sit on the Porters' curb and wait until the other showed up to sit and talk on the edge of the streetlight's glow. No parents involved. The Porters didn't seem to mind.

"Why? He already kicked my ass."

"I guess he doesn't remember it well enough. Maybe he wants to relive the glory of kicking the ass of Bad-Boy Ronnie Brown."

Ronnie snorted. "Yeah, maybe not enough people saw it."

"Just stay away from him for awhile, okay? Everybody knows he's got a short attention span. He'll be onto some other grudge any day now."

"I don't get it. What grudge does he have with me?"

"Ronnie, Ronnie . . . you're still expecting the world to make sense, poor boy."

The previous year the Roscoe twins had nearly raped her. She'd gone to their house when their parents were out for the night because she had a crush on Bill Roscoe. She'd gotten drunk on their parents' liquor, and the twins had pinned her down. She said she had to pee, and they let her up. She ran home and knocked on the basement window and got Ronnie up, and he snuck her down the stairs. She showed him the bruises on her arms. She lifted her jean skirt to show him the red handprint on her thigh. He was both horrified and furious. His bad advice had been to say nothing, that he'd take care of it. On Monday, the story in school was that they'd taken turns with her. She showed her bruises to girls in the bathroom, so at least they knew the truth. Alfonso had gotten into it, volunteering to help Ronnie take on the Roscoe twins, who were not particularly tough. The Roscoes lived in the new subdivision with bigger houses on the other side of Ten Mile Road, further from Detroit. He and Alfonso had jumped them in the parking lot, but the security guard and the auto shop teacher quickly pulled them apart. Beneath the deeper pain she was feeling, Carol had either been angry with him or pleased or both. Ronnie could never quite tell.

Ronnie looked up at her and swallowed. "Yeah, sorry. I forgot."

"You forgot?"

"I mean, I forgot it doesn't have to make sense. I didn't forget what happened."

"Just watch your back, tough guy."

She kissed his cheek and headed back into her house. The confab was over. He had wanted to tell her about his latest meeting with Alfonso's father, another thing that made no sense. Maybe she could explain to him why he liked sitting on the heated seat while they discussed murder.

It was only early April, but the weather was all wacky, and it felt like summer, the kind of summer they saw on TV shows filmed in California. The sun yellow, the sky blue, with a few wispy clouds drifting around the edges like the shy and sober at a high school dance. Even the wind had died down. Spring break had just started, and Ronnie was taking last year's Christmas lights out of the bushes out front. He could barely look up at that sky, but when he did raise his head, he saw the dark glow, the pure spotless sheen of Mr. Cardenal's car down the street. He didn't remember ever seeing it in the light of day, in all its menacing substance, on a street of Impalas and Escorts and minivans, and even the rare Corvette or Mustang driven by an upstart drug dealer. Ronnie was sure Alfonso's father knew exactly who drove what and who was into what shit, though why would he be out here in the afternoon, clearly visible to all, including his ex?

Ronnie dropped his strings of lights and headed down the street. When he got close to the car, Mr. Cardenal's large curly head popped out the open window like a jacked-up jack-in-the-box.

"Hey, Junior," he said, smiling and squinting up at Ronnie in a familiar way, as if he was expecting him. "Waiting on Alfonso," he nodded toward the house. "She's letting me take him to the beach."

"You get vacations in your line of work?" Ronnie asked. For his spring break, he'd taken on some extra hours working at the Unimart, his after-school job.

"Ain't no vacation," he replied.

"Hmph," Ronnie said. "Who washes your car? It's like, perfect." He smiled and gently grazed his fingers over the hood.

"I've got this guy down in the city who works for my boss—he's an artist. He assures me that every grain of Florida sand will slide right off. Go ahead and try and sit on it."

Ronnie hesitated. He looked up for Alfonso, who never mentioned his father in his long, rambling monologues on the way to school about who kicked whose ass and what girls were currently chasing him, how he had to beat them off with a stick. Ronnie imagined Alfonso in a bathing suit, the ribs lined up like speed bumps across his hollow sternum. Some refugee from an African country, like in those hunger posters, though Alfonso was white, and any starving going on was of his own doing.

"Go ahead."

Ronnie jumped on the hood and slid right off, hitting his ass on the bumper on his way down. Mr. Cardenal howled with laughter. He seemed hyper about the trip with Alfonso. Maybe even nervous. Ronnie picked himself up. He turned and nodded at Mr. Cardenal. "Slick," he said, rubbing his sore tailbone.

Alfonso's father winked at him. "Hey," he half whispered. "Keep an eye on the house." He jerked his head toward where Alfonso was dragging a lime-green suitcase down the driveway. "If you know what I mean." Ronnie waved to Alfonso, who was wearing wraparound sunglasses. His father was squinting. Ronnie wondered about that. Shouldn't the gangster be wearing the shades?

"I never know what you mean," Ronnie said.

"There will be something in it for you," Mr. Cardenal said. "You know what that means, don't you?"

Alfonso approached the car, out of breath. Ronnie turned to face him. "Don't get sunburned, dude," he said. He stopped himself from punching Alfonso's glass shoulder. "What you got in that suitcase, bricks?"

"You and my dad buddies now?" Alfonso said. He looked like he'd caught them at something illicit. "That's sick."

"Just exchanging notes on the time of day," Mr. Cardenal said pleasantly. He popped the trunk for Alfonso. Ronnie glanced at the immaculate and empty trunk, then hurried off down the street. Whatever Mr. Cardenal was doing, he was traveling light. No suitcases, no dead bodies.

During spring break, Ronnie took to circling the block, taking the long way home past the Cardenal house. After work, he was out every night, looking for the elusive party that would welcome him. No school meant more parties. Ed bought beer for him, because someone had bought beer for *him* when he was Ronnie's age, and because they had no father who might have weighed in on the matter. Their father married their mother because he got her pregnant with Ed while on leave after basic training. His Uncle Bob had told them this one night at his daughter Lil's wedding, held under similar circumstances. "No disrespect to your dear mother," he'd said, his eyes bloodshot as he leaned into Ed and Ronnie over the cheap paper tablecloth in their grade school cafeteria, all of the wedding guests gigantic and sad at the tiny tables in the strange sour antiseptic air that all the whiskey in the world couldn't mask.

Ronnie missed Mr. Cardenal. He missed the chance of seeing him, the presence of the gun, the elegance of the heated seats, and the tanklike aura of that solid car. He felt protected with Mr. Cardenal, even while they discussed murder.

When he cased the Cardenal's house, he imagined himself a secret agent or scout back in the Wild West. He squirmed behind bushes on his belly. He pulled himself above cement ledges to peer into windows. A green Cadillac was parked in the driveway nearly every night that week, behind Mrs. Alfonso's mother's golden Cougar. Even when it wasn't, Ronnie still had a quick look around. He hadn't been in Alfonso's house since they were in junior high and he'd knocked a half-eaten apple into one of the pockets of their pool table through sheer brilliant stupidity. They shoved all of the balls into the pocket, trying to dislodge the apple, but it just got wedged in tighter.

Mrs. Cardenal had motherfucked him out the door, and he'd never returned. Alfonso said she'd had to call his father, something she hated doing. He sent over a man who had to take the whole table apart. Ronnie had never brought that up to Mr. Cardenal. Surely, if he thought Ronnie was the one who nearly ruined a simple pool table, he wouldn't have asked him to kill his wife.

The Cardenals' was the only house within miles to have a pool table. The basement walls were dark with mold, the bare light bulbs dim, the washer and dryer rocked and thumped nearby. But it was theirs—the house with the pool table. They could've received mail addressed to the House With the Pool Table, Warren, MI, and it would have arrived. It must've taken some doing to get it down the narrow basement steps. Mrs. Cardenal, who didn't even play pool, would never relinquish it.

The story was that Mr. Cardenal had won it in a poker game. Or maybe it was payment for a debt. It had a coin slot, so it must've come from a bar or pool hall. Ronnie never did find out exactly what Mr. Cardenal's job was with the vegetable-shop mob.

From his comfortable perch on top of the back fence, Ronnie could look through the dining room window, into the living room and kitchen, and get a glimpse Mrs. Cardenal's bedroom. When it was just Mrs. Cardenal, the view was like a boring sitcom. He marveled at how the object of her ex husband's obsession could seem so ordinary, sitting blankly in front of the TV set. He took a strange comfort in observing another house besides his own where no man was present.

Ronnie's father had been killed in the Vietnam War when Ronnie was still in his mother's womb. Ed was only three, so he also had no memory of their father. It had happened so long ago that none of his friends ever mentioned it. It was part of the street's lore—the House Where the Guy Got Killed in Vietnam. But that sign had faded over the years. It didn't have the slightly illicit allure of the Cardenals' pool table. Ronnie's mother had never remarried, though she sometimes did not come home at night now that the boys were in high school. She always let them know. She told them she'd only bring somebody home if it was serious, and in all the years, she had brought no one.

When a remarkably pale Alfonso returned from Florida, Ronnie began carrying his notes with him at all times, expecting to run into Mr. Cardenal at any turn of the corner onto Funke Street, but the blue Town Car did not reappear for weeks. Ronnie suspected foul play and decided to keep up the spying. He knew who slept where and what they did when they were not sleeping.

One night after their return, Ronnie sat at a basement well window watching Alfonso shoot pool for hours. Alfonso was good. Better than good. He methodically circled the table, knocking the balls in one after the other. Ronnie found himself rooting for Alfonso. It was a world where everything

26

stayed in its place until Alfonso decided otherwise. Ronnie let himself feel sympathy for his childhood friend, living in that house alone with his crazy mother, who during the summer roamed the street in a gold metal flake bikini and sunned herself in the driveway, coated in baby oil, glistening, a gaudy star on a tarnished street. No wonder Mr. Cardenal was crazy with hatred and longing.

"So, what exactly does your mother do?" Ronnie once asked Alfonso. "I mean, besides get a tan?"

Carol snorted.

"Don't mess with my moms," Alfonso said, "You know better than that. She'll kick your ass, pool-table boy."

Carol snorted again.

"One bad apple. Still busting my chops over one bad apple."

They all broke into laughter.

"She works out of the house," Alfonso said mysteriously, raising his eyebrows in what looked more like sadness than secret knowledge.

Ronnie thought about making a wisecrack, but he just looked at Carol and rolled his eyes. Behind Alfonso, Carol pushed her hands up under her breasts and stuck her tongue out in imitation of Mrs. Cardenal. Ronnie laughed. Alfonso whirled around and caught her.

"In your dreams, Carol, in your dreams," he said to her.

"In my dreams, what, Alfonso?" she asked. "You don't know shit about my dreams."

"He was . . . exquisite," Ronnie told Carol, and she scoffed.

"Exquisite? Have you been using the dictionary again? I warned you about that. . . . Alfonso, a pool shark, who woulda thunk it."

Mrs. Porter was cleaning her windows, and they could hear the paper towels squeaking against glass as they sat on the curb.

"Yeah, I know. He was never that good back when—"

"You mean, B.A., before apple?"

Ronnie looked at her and shook his head. "It's like he's a human pool cue. Come watch him sometime."

"Ronnie, you're getting a little weird on me. Why don't you go back to getting drunk every night—I understood you better then."

"You ever in a car with heated seats?" he asked.

"Are you coming onto me, Ronnie Brown?"

"No, a real car where the seats heat up your butt."

"My butt doesn't get cold," she said. "My hands get cold, and my feet get cold, and my ears get cold. My fucking *butt* doesn't get cold. Sounds kinky," she said.

"They're great. I hear they're great," he found himself saying. The way she put it, he couldn't bring himself to fill in the gaps in the Cardenal story. The gun, the proposal. Carol thought him keeping an eye on Mrs. Cardenal was weird enough all by itself.

One night, Ronnie saw Alfonso dressed in drag. He jumped down off the fence and snuck up to push his face against the window. His heart thumped loud in his chest. He wanted to change the channel, erase the screen, shamed by witnessing his old friend's private perversion. Alfonso preened in front of a full-length mirror in the hallway in one of his mother's miniskirts, watching himself dance. An odd lump of grief sat in Ronnie's gut. Grief for the rest of Alfonso's life and night's sad drift that would lead him to exposure, exile. What would either of his parents have to say about that? Ronnie could not bear it. He slunk off toward home.

He wanted to tell Carol, but it was too late to sit in front of the Porters. Too late to call. And what would he say, what would he expect from her, from burdening her with a secret neither of them could absorb. Funke Street did not allow such behavior. The wind scoured bricks. The wind kept heads lowered. Ronnie went home and lay in bed long after his brother had left for work. He wrote nothing down in his notebook for Mr. Cardenal. That morning, Carol and Alfonso walked to school without him as Ronnie tried to sleep off the bad liquor of what he'd seen.

When the Town Car finally did reappear, one midnight in late May, Ronnie had stopped carrying his notes.

"What's the deal?" Ronnie said immediately after Mr. Cardenal rolled down his window, idling not in front of his old house but closer to Ronnie's, down by the corner. He tilted his head out the window. His clothes were uncharacteristically disheveled, and he smelled like smoke and whiskey. If he'd gotten any color in Florida, something had drained it out of him.

Ronnie had his speech rehearsed. "You hired me to keep an eye on the house while you were gone, and I did. I got notes. Dates and times, the works, and then you don't show up. You should pay me for what—"

"He's fucking her on the table, isn't he?"

"What?"

"You heard me. Is he or is he not fucking her on my pool table?"

"I never seen that."

"You never seen that?" Mr. Cardenal said, cruelly mocking him. He had lost all the cool reserve that Ronnie had admired. "What did you see, then, before I go paying you?"

"I don't have my notes—they're back at my house. Where you been? You drunk?"

"Notes? Is it that fucking complicated you need notes?"

"If you're gonna kill her, you need dates, times, patterns," Ronnie said.

Mr. Cardenal winced. "I thought *you* were gonna kill her, my friend."

Ronnie forced a harsh laugh. "Why you always calling me your friend?"

"Just tell me what you saw." His head lolled low against the window.

Ronnie groaned. This wasn't going how he'd imagined. "Same guy, every night. Not the one with my uncle's car. This guy, he's got greasy hair, combed straight back like a punk. Walks like he's got a stick up his ass. He's keeping clothes there, man. I think he's half moved in. . . . You're paying me, right?"

"Half moved in? That clown's married," Mr. Cardenal closed his eyes. "Shit. It's Ricky Dude, the cock of the fucking walk."

"He don't look married."

"Kid, he wears a wedding ring. Probably doesn't even take it off to fuck my wife." He looked at Ronnie as he emphasized *wife*.

"I never thought . . ."

"You never thought. You got to think."

"I don't know anybody who's married. Not even my ma. What finger you wear a wedding ring on?"

"You're killing me, kid, killing me." He surprised Ronnie by sliding his hand out the window and waving his left hand in the air, where the thick gold ring glistened in the light.

"Your ma—she wear her ring?"

Ronnie knew he should know, but he tried to picture his mother's hands and could not.

"I don't think so."

Mr. Cardenal sighed. "That was a stupid fucking war. You know that, right?"

Ronnie never thought much about that war, any war. "Did you fight in it?" Mr. Cardenal must have been close to Ronnie's father's age. He felt an odd tug on his heart, a weight. "Did you fight in it too?"

Mr. Cardenal sneered. "I wasn't no chump—no offense, I understand your father had other issues. My family took care of me. I got me a lucky number in that lottery, if you know what I mean."

Ronnie didn't. He looked up at his own house, the unkempt yard and peeling paint. He felt guilty for not being a man, not taking care of things. He and his brother, they were just biding time till they left that house in shambles.

Mr. Cardenal pulled his head in the window and leaned it back against the headrest, reclining the seat slowly with the automatic control. "Okay, my friend, my secret spy guy, tell me something I don't already know about 3612 Funke Street."

"He—he dresses in women's clothing."

"What?" Mr. Cardenal roared forward in his seat.

"Just kidding," Ronnie said. "Gotcha, didn't I?"

"You're a pervert. . . . How many times they do it every night?"

"See, that's what I need my notes for," Ronnie said. He didn't want to go into the details of his voyeurism, his shamed excitement at watching live sex when he himself had yet to experience it.

"Oh God," Mr. Cardenal said. "He needs notes for this. It's either once or twice, right? It's gotta be just once or twice, I mean, the guy's—"

"I don't know when one time stops and the next time starts." Both their faces were flaming red.

"I saw him leave a wad of money on the table once," Ronnie said quickly, hoping to steer away from the actual sex.

"He's paying her? My wife's—"

"Ex wife." Ronnie couldn't help himself.

"—taking money to sleep with Ricky the Dude, husband of Licky?"

"Licky the Dude?"

"Licky—that's what we call her. Long story." Mr. Cardenal waved his hand in the air. He was holding the gun loose in his grip, as if unaware it was even there.

"No wonder you want to kill him."

"Her. I want to kill her. Him, he's not worth it." Mr. Cardenal spit a healthy gob out the window. Ronnie felt a slight spray against his arm and backed away. "It's her. I can't stand her being alive like this."

Mr. Cardenal shook in his seat, trying to contain his raw grief and rage. "Are they doing dope or something? What's going on in her head?"

"I ain't seen no dope, and I know something about dope," Ronnie said importantly.

"You mean pot, kid. I'm talking pills and shit."

"Everybody takes pills. My mom takes pills."

"Your mother . . ." Mr. Cardenal said. "Jesus Christ, Ricky the Dude."

"And his wife, Licky. . . . Gimme the money. I'll get the notes. It's not like you don't know where to find me."

"You know why I wasn't coming by?"

Ronnie looked down the empty street, the car's hot exhaust drifting up toward him. He shook his head.

"I thought I was getting over it. Got out of town with the boy, did some gambling down at the jai alai places. They call them frontons—is that a weird word or what? Eating good food—Chinese, Cuban. Alfonso playing video games. Laying in the sun, and that ocean sound, you know—whoosh—the hot sand, some friends from the business, guys who don't know about all this, you know. . . . Then I come back and it's like the street lost its magnet and I'm just not pulled, I'm free, then today I see her getting in her car down outside Carlo's Roadside. Somewhere she *knows* I spend time. Got magnetized all over again."

"Jai alai? That some martial arts shit?"

Mr. Alfonso laughed loud and abrupt, like he was barking. Ronnie thought he was going to spit on him again, so he backed off.

"It's a sport. A Miami sport. They whip this ball two hundred miles an hour against a wall."

"So you magnetized again, huh? Think you should be driving with all that magnetic shit going on?"

"What happened to the days you were afraid of me? Alfonso's afraid of me, and I don't even want him to be. You, you should be afraid of me." He paused. "You are the Apple Boy. . . ." Mr. Cardenal jabbed the gun into the air in Ronnie's general direction. "You owe me, Apple Boy."

"You even got bullets for that thing?" Ronnie asked. "It was an accident."

"You don't need bullets," he said. "You'll understand someday." He winked at Ronnie, and Ronnie flinched.

"How you gonna kill your wife without bullets?"

Ronnie had more to say, but Mr. Cardenal's eyes were tearing up. He stared straight out the window as if he was driving, in motion, being pulled forward by a force Ronnie had yet to experience.

A black plastic garbage bag snagged on a picker bush blew and danced in the wind as if alive, occasionally thunking when a big gust inflated it like a balloon. Funke Street was a horizontal flow that carried everything and everyone until they stuck on something. They spent the rest of their lives trying to decide whether to continue hanging on or try to disentangle themselves from whatever had hooked them. Ronnie didn't know whether he was hooked yet, or whether he wanted to be.

Six months later, Alfonso died in a sledding accident. It shocked everyone—particularly the fact that it was an accident and not some health problem. He'd crashed into the one big tree at the bottom of the one sledding hill within a dozen miles—a man-made one constructed of landfill trash. Suicide by sledding? By stupidity?

When he heard the news, Ronnie ran outside. Carol was already sitting on the curb between parked cars in front of the Porters' house, away from the adults who wanted to comfort her. They watched the lit windows of Alfonso's mother's house down the street. Occasionally, a shadow slipped by the curtained front window. They could hear nothing but the hiss of cars from the distant freeway. Carol wiped away a couple of silent tears.

Ronnie asked her to go with him to see Alfonso in the funeral home.

"With you? That sounds weird, like a date or something."

"You remember how we used to ditch Alfonso?"

"Why did he want to be with us anyway?"

"He thought we were cool."

"He's ditched *us* now, eh? . . . Sure, Ronnie, I'll go with you."

"With Alfonso on the street, I never had to worry about being the biggest asshole. Know what I mean?"

"What time do you go to these things?"

"When it opens, I guess. Nah—we don't want to be too early. It might just be his family, and that'd be weird," Ronnie said, thinking it'd be weirder than weird. "I'll stop by and get you."

"You gonna ride me over on your handlebars, like the old days?"

"How can I look up your skirt if you're on my handlebars?"

"You say the sweetest things," she said. "7:30. Fashionably late. Ha." But neither of them laughed.

Ronnie tried to exhale a deep breath, but it stuttered on the way out. "I don't think there's fashionable when it comes to funerals. My mom went out to get me a tie."

"Get out."

"No, really,"

"This I gotta see—Ronnie Brown in a tie. . . . Alfonso, man, he's already missing so much." Carol began to sob, and Ronnie awkwardly put his arms around her, their puffy down coats rubbing against each other like air hissing out of tires.

Ronnie had never just hugged anybody except as a quick step to making out. He kissed her dirty blonde hair. He stared down, losing himself in her dark roots.

"I know somebody named Licky," he said. "Maybe she'll be there."

"A fucking sled kills him. One tree on the whole damn hill," Mr. Cardenal whispered hoarsely, as if pleading for it not to be so. Dressed in an elegant blue suit, he stood in the parking lot chewing an unlit cigar. His face looked like a withered plant, his dark complexion faded out, his eyes slack, black, sunken.

"I bought him that sled when he was eight."

Ronnie and Carol looked at each other. They remembered the sled, lying on top of each other, going down, sprawling in the up-spray of snow, Alfonso whining, "It's mine, you guys," till they finally gave him a turn on his own sled. Ronnie pictured the hill—it'd be impossible to hit that tree by accident. Unless you wanted to see how close you could get, just for the thrill.

"Just forget about that other stuff," Mr. Cardenal said quietly, his voice quivering. He put his arms around Ronnie and gave him a big, long, awkward hug.

Carol gave them a funny look and slunk off to join the small cluster of other neighborhood kids smoking cigarettes in the cold.

"Have you been inside yet?" Ronnie heard someone ask her.

"I wasn't gonna kill nobody," Ronnie whispered into the cologne or deodorant of Mr. Cardenal, smelling nice for his son's funeral.

"I know, son, I know. Neither was I," he sighed, and Ronnie felt the absence of the gun as the big man held him tight and slipped something in his pocket.

Ronnie and Carol walked into the ornate foyer. Though it was warm inside, the marble statues gave him a chill.

"Looks like we're in ancient Rome or something," Carol said.

"Isn't that where they fed people to the lions?" Ronnie said.

"Alfonso's already been fed to the lions," she said.

"We gotta go in," Ronnie said, loosening his tie, then tightening it again.

Together they entered the viewing room behind the small sign with Alfonso's name in stick-on letters. Ronnie noticed they had spelled "Cardenal" "Cardinal."

It looked like they'd plumped up Alfonso, like they'd stuffed the Scarecrow. Ronnie held Carol's hand as they knelt on the padded kneelers in front of the flower-drenched casket.

The vegetable-market Mafioso were there, speaking in a low hum, feet planted in a wide stance in support of one of their own.

Ronnie mumbled odd snatches of prayer, strung them together in a ragged stream: "Our Father, Glory be, full of grace, forgive us our trespasses, of thy fruit among women, bless me for I have sinned. Peace be with you, Alfonso."

Carol shook her hand free. She grabbed the edge of the coffin and held on. Ronnie closed his eyes. He'd seen enough of Alfonso dead. Finally, Carol rose, and he rose with her. A subtle line of mourners waited behind them to take their places as they hurried outside again.

Now only the funeral home director, Mr. Lombardo, stood in the cold. He held the door for them under the covered entranceway.

"The family appreciates you paying your respects," he said.

"Oh, we ain't done paying 'em," Carol said.

"Learn how to spell, old man," Ronnie said.

After a quick, shared cigarette, they reentered, Mr. Lombardo sighing at them like didn't they know the etiquette of paying respects. They paused in the pale, hollow foyer. The door of the other viewing room was propped open, and through the narrow gap Ronnie glimpsed Mr. Cardenal's thick, round back. He drifted toward the dim slice of light.

"Where you going, Ron?" Carol asked. He thought of what it meant that she called him Ron, not Ronnie. "Alfonso's over here," she said, pointing to the next room.

It was like they were playing a childhood game, and she'd found his hiding place. Her voice was high, shrill, and wavering. He took her hand and motioned for her to be quiet.

Inside the empty room, folding chairs lined neatly in the back of the room awaited the next victim of the lions. Mr. Cardenal and his ex wife, Pepper, stood together. His head leaned heavily down onto her shoulder. She looked almost staggered with the weight, but she seemed determined to hold on, bracing herself, a long leg extended behind her for support.

Ronnie knew he was spying again. Grief held him, and he held Carol. "Oh, God," she whispered. Someone tapped on Ronnie's shoulder. "Excuse me," he said, and Ronnie knew as soon as he turned that it was the other man, the lover, the guy in the green Cadillac, license plate MNS 437. He pushed past them and closed the door in their faces.

They backed away. "Ricky the Dude with clothes on. This might get interesting," Ronnie said. "Or maybe just sadder." But in a few seconds, Ricky rushed out of the room, slamming the door behind him. "Shit," he spat, and headed straight for the exit.

"What's going on?" Carol asked. She looked tiny in the big fancy black dress her mother had purchased for her. Alfonso probably would've liked that too. His old mud-pie pals dressed like dolls for his funeral. Ronnie felt like they were shrinking into tiny plastic action figures with no one there to provide the action. He grabbed her and kissed her hard. "Shit," she said, catching her breath.

"Is that all anybody can say is 'shit'?"

"It was a positive 'shit,'" she said. "A surprised where-did-that-come-from 'shit.'"

"I didn't know what else to do," he said, a little too loud. "He wanted me to kill her," he said softly, "but it was a half-want. It was a love-want."

"You're talking crazy," she said, squeezing his arm.

"Yeah, I know," he said. "I think I need to kiss you again."

They hurried into the cold, past Mr. Lombardo's muted groan and into the parking lot out back. As Ronnie pulled his sport coat tight around him, he felt a crinkling in his pocket. An envelope fell out onto the ground. Carol bent over and picked it up. She peeked inside.

"Hey," Ronnie said, surprised as she pulled out a handful of twenties.

"Hey yourself," she said. "What's this, blood money?"

"It's the opposite of blood money," he said. "It's Monopoly money—but I think I'll keep it."

"Will you take me out to dinner?" she asked, leaning into him. "We can be like grown-ups and shit. We can drink wine and tell stories about our old friend Alfonso."

"Grown-ups are too nuts. Let's not be grown-ups yet. We'll wear these outfits to the fucking prom."

"Yeah," Carol said, and stomped her hard heel on the pavement. "The fucking prom. We can get drunk and puke all over our fancy clothes."

Ronnie laughed, a laugh heavy with grief and love and compassion and all unspoken things.

"We have to figure out how to get to school from now on."

"I'll hold your hand."

She laughed. "No, you won't."

"I'll tell you about all the girls fighting over me."

"No, you won't."

"I'll tell you how I once got an apple stuck in a pool table. I'll tell you about the time Alfonso's mom bent over in her metal-flake bikini and I saw her tit."

"She only has one?"

"I only saw one. That was enough."

"She wanted to kill you about that apple."

"Wanting and doing are two different things."

"Ronnie, I want you. Are you gonna do anything about it?"

When they turned the corner around the building and into the parking lot, the first car they saw was the Lincoln—in a spot reserved for grieving families, Ronnie guessed.

He lifted Carol onto the hood. She slid into him as he kissed her hard. He wanted their bones to touch somewhere. He felt the warmth of her thighs enclosing his. They heard the hard clicking of dress shoes against the asphalt parking lot draw close, then pass.

"Disgraceful," a woman muttered, and Ronnie knew she was right. But how do you honor the dead, he wondered as they broke the kiss and simply held each other again like the old friends they were. Disgraceful, but perhaps Mr. Cardenal would not mind, being no stranger to disgrace, being no stranger to the odd, twisted roads of grief and healing.

Ronnie decided that he would wash and wax Mr. Cardenal's car for him, so shiny he could see his own face. So they could all see their own faces.

CLOWN, DROWN

Robert Holmes
English 101
MCCC
"Dying is Not Funny"
First draft

I've been wanting to write about this all semester, but I'm worried that your just going to laugh. It sounds like the punch line of a bad joke. It even rhymes: clown, drown. But I know I'm supposed to write about things that changed my life, and this qualifies (right, teach?).

At the thirteenth annual Southeastern Michigan Clown Convention (we call it a convention so we can write it off our taxes. It's more of a reunion/ party. No agenda, breakout sessions, panel discussions, etc. After all, we're clowns, right?) at this resort Up North, Carl's Kabins, this clown from Sterling Heights fell out of a rowboat and drown. I was in the boat with him, and I should of been able to save him. This nawing thought keeps me awake at night, and it has effected my clowning business. Thus, I am back at school at the ripe old age of thirty-three, the age at which many clowns are just coming into there own.

There's more male clowns than female clowns at these things. I don't know why clowning got to be mostly a guy thing. I know more woman are getting into it, but on the birthday circuit, the kids just don't seem to relate to woman clowns. I think it's too much like there Ma. A male clown is usually nothing like their dads, who never come to the parties anyway. Being a clown is generally considered whimpy, at least in my old neighborhood. When I started clowning, everybody acted like I'd come out as gay or something.

The clown who drowned was an ordained minister who lost his congregation. They voted him out, not for being a clown, but for being gay. He use to do all these religious funraisers. Clowning for Christ. You maybe read about him in the papers. Being a clown makes it easy to change your name and your looks, and that's what allowed him to continue working as a clown (he had a clown makeover). He didn't abuse any kids or nothing like that. His partner (that's what they call them) had a sex-change operation and—well, it's hard to keep that kind of thing secret, so the church axed him.

We always had our convention during the week so nobody would lose any gigs, and plus we could get a deal on lodgings. We'd been going to the same place for—well, I started going in the eighth year—every year up near Traverse City, but it was getting too hotsy-totsy up there, and they priced us out. Somebody came up with this "Carl's" place. It was our first (and last) time there. I mean, "Kabins?" Even I know that's spelled wrong.

The dead clown's real name was Everett, but his clown name was Fun House (his second clown name). I thought it was catchy. My name is Rocko Socko—I went macho. This is Detroit, what was I gonna do, be Clarence or something?

We're not a bunch of freaks. I know there's this whole thing about kids being afraid of clowns, etc., but most of us are pretty normal. The only thing I notice is that a lot of clowns smoke. I don't know why that is. Anyway, what I'm saying is we didn't walk around all weekend in our clown get-ups. Just for the Saturday night party.

Carl's was a dump, but they had a nice fire pit. We got a keg and set up a bar on a picnic table. The owner (Carl, I guess) didn't seem to much care what we did as long as we paid in cash (this turned out to be a bit of a problem, since the other place took credit cards, but we found an ATM with old Carl's help).

My wife never came to these clown things. Some people brought their spouses, but usually only once. I think they felt like outsiders, even without us being in make-up and all. My wife wanted to know what I was doing in a rowboat at 3 A.M. with Fun, the gay clown. (You know, he might of been able to make that as his gimmick, just like the Jesus thing, but I'm not sure there's such a market in the gay community.)

In terms of how it effected my life, my wife left me after this. Luckily, we didn't have any kids. Why did she leave me? It depends on how I tell the story. I didn't tell the story right, and that's why she left. I should of just told her what I told the police. (Should I save this for my conclusion?)

It was an odd night. It had rained all day, and then finally stopped. Old Carl kept dry wood under a tarp, so that was no problem. The air smelled like rotting wood. (No, that's to close to the other wood. Similes—I call them smiles—should be further apart, right?). How about, the air smelled like dirt? Smelled like somebody was going to die? I can't describe it, but I smelled the same smell since then, after a good rain. It's something the rain sets off, not rain itself. Because of the rain, some of the clowns decided not to do the make-up, so we had half clowns and half not clowns. I myself was in my clown gear. Seeing as I was one of the younger clowns, I thought it might be disrespectful, arrogant even, to not dress up. The cabins had bad lighting and old, cloudy mirrors, but a lot of us brought our own make-up mirrors. Never count on anything being on location.

Fun and I had known each other a few years. A lot of us car-pooled up together, since we were all coming from the same part of the state, so we'd shared a car a couple of years, but not last year. Last year he came alone for some reason.

We were standing around the fire. My make-up was all sticky. Fun had his make-up on too. It was like on one side of the fire were the people in costume, and on the other half, the people in jeans and jackets (it was a little cold out). Nobody said anything about it until Fun just says—this is after a few trips to the keg—says kind of loud, "I guess I'd just feel naked without my face on."

Then, somebody says "You sound like a woman." Then somebody else says something smart to mock Fun for being gay. Not like anybody called him a fag or anything, just sort of exaggerating what he said, and doing that gay wave thing, but then I guess he was inspired or something—this was one of the old-school clowns, Bippo, who claimed he toured with Barnum once—he makes the Sign of the Cross in that swishy wave, and that just does it for Fun.

I'm standing right next to him, so I see his shoulders start to shake like he's laughing, but he's really starting to cry. He's not making any noise. It's like he's miming crying, but tears are coming down his cheeks. Yeah, yeah, "The Tears of a Clown" I know. But there WAS someone around, and everybody starts in on each other, and the women clowns are really sticking up for Fun, which in some ways makes it worse.

I went and put my arm around him. "Fun," I said. "Fuck the marshmallows tonight, let's go for a walk." (I figure its okay to swear when people are talking because that's the way they talk. Am I using quotations marks right?) We always had marshmallows. It was a jokey thing, with everybody looking for the best stick and everything. Clowns can be very serious about clowning, but the reason they became clowns in the first place has to do with wanting to be like a kid. At least, I think so.

At the last gathering in Traverse City, someone had thrown Bippo's orange wig into the fire and caused a scene resulting in an apology and replacement wig, so Bippo was even more of a blowhard than usual that weekend as some kind of compensation. Like, he was going to make sure he wasn't the one laughed at this year.

I wasn't wearing my floppy oversized shoes. Too muddy. But Fun had his on, so as I led him away, I realized that we couldn't walk far. Carl had a couple of rowboats he left anchored on shore. He had a dock, but that was for his motorboat, which we weren't allowed to use.

"How about a little row then?" I said.

Fun hiccupped and nodded, so I pulled the anchor out of the wet sand and through it into the boat. Fun slowly climbed in, and I pushed us off and into the water, then hopped in. Because of the rain, the bottom of the boat had a good inch or two of water sloshing around down there. Fun put his big feet up on the edge of the boat so he wouldn't ruin his shoes. I started rowing, and the oars squeaked in their—what do you call those things the oars go into, oar holders?

"Look at those clowns," somebody shouted from shore. It was an old joke, but everybody laughed.

"Damn right," I shouted back, and everybody laughed again, and I was sure everything was going to be okay by the time Fun and I got back.

We got out aways onto the small lake. Tea Lake. Probably because the water was kind of brown. The clown bonfire looked a bit odd from a distance, the little flashes of bright make-up and hair, like it was some wierd cult thing, when it was just a bunch of clowns getting hammered. It felt good to be away from them.

"Thanks, Rocco," Fun said. He'd calmed down, but he still looked like one sad little clown sitting there.

"Shit, I said, we should of brought the fishing stuff. We could catch some clown-fish." (I know, Fun groaned too). But I was a little giddy to be out in the rowboat in the dark. I'd never done that before. The sky opened up above us with a lot more stars than we're use to in the city. A slice of moon was low on the horizon.

"Nights like this," Fun said. He sighed and pulled out a pack of cigarettes (he sowed a pocket for smokes on the inside of the costume). He offered me one, and the big magic sky with the water lapping gently against the boat made me take one.

Fun was a puppet clown. He had a whole suitcase full of puppets that he took on gigs. He could throw his voice pretty good. His audience was preschoolers mostly. I got mostly the kids who were half in on the joke already. The kids who were too old for clowns, but their moms got them one any way. I did juggling and card tricks mostly. We all did balloon animals. If you couldn't do balloon animals, you may as well be busking as a mime or some lame stuff like that.

"This could be a romantic night. It has romantic potential," Fun said.

I didn't know how to take that. "Yeah, if you were with the right person," I said, though to be honest, I wasn't imagining my wife as the right person at that moment. I was thinking about this school teacher who'd hired me for their spring fair a couple of months before.

"Edwina left me," Fun said.

Edwina aka Edwin was the sex-change recipient. I had imagined that kind of irrevocable gesture meant some kind of irrevocable love, but I guess I was wrong.

"For—you're gonna love this—another woman," Fun looked like he was going to start that heaving thing again, so I stopped rowing and put my hand on his shoulder. I didn't know what to say to that weird kind of betrayal. I couldn't even figure it out.

"What do you think God makes of all that?" I asked. I was more comfortable going with God than with the gay stuff.

"The thing about God is that he doesn't get erections, so he doesn't understand any of this," Fun said.

"Is that in the Bible?" I asked.

"People don't get it. The Bible is this big blank book. You can read anything into it, and it becomes true."

Another boat passed us then, a lantern in the front. It looked like a father and son going fishing.

"How they biting?" the man asked.

Fun and I looked at each other, our faces masked by clown emotions.

"Great," I kind of whispered. "They're biting like crazy." The old man had his back to us as he rowed, his broad shoulders pulling against the oars like he could row forever. His son got a good look at us, but the boy said nothing.

"After a good rain," the man said, than his words trailed off into the night.

I started rowing again in the opposite direction, and I realized I'd lost sight of the clown campfire.

"Fun, do you know where we are?" I asked.

"Call me Everett," he said.

"You know, sometimes my puppets have minds of their own," he said. And he lifted his hands in the air like they had puppets on them, though they did not.

What happened next?

I shoved Fun away when he grabbed my crotch, and his shoe caught on the bench in the middle of the boat, and the whole thing flipped over. I knew enough to rip off everything I could as I sank to the bottom—the wig, the baggy outfit, my sneakers. I splashed back to the surface, gasping for air. I started immediately swimming in the direction of the closest lights on shore, then caught myself.

I turned and shouted, "Fun," and the sound echoed across the water. I guess whoever heard it didn't think much—it was a Friday night.

"Fun!" I shouted again. In the darkness, I heard no splashing, no crying out. Was he hanging onto the capsized boat? "Fun!" I shouted, then finally thought to yell "Help!"

I yelled "Help!" then swam the rest of the way to shore.

I crawled out of the mucky sand near two old couples sitting around a campfire.

"Well, if it ain't the creature from the black lagoon!" One guy said, they were drunk. It was one of those lakes surrounded by drunks. They were no help. By the time the county police got their boat in the water, it was nearly dawn and they were just looking for the body.

All morning, the rest of the clowns stood with me on shore waiting for word (none of them in clown gear at that point). They did not blame me, though old Carl, you could tell he was thinking about the bad publicity, about getting sued, not some dead clown who would never make anyone laugh ever again.

I told the police that he was drunk and fell out of the boat and tipped it over. I told them I couldn't find him, and all that's true. They finally found his body right before dark the next day. The lake wasn't that big.

Things hadn't been great with my wife at that point anyways. She was the steady bread-winner, as they say, working as a secretary at the local grade school. She didn't think it was so cute, me being a clown anymore. When we got married, I think she'd imagined it more of a temporary thing. See, and that affected everything else, you know, all the personal stuff. I got my health benefits through her, so I'm currently doing without.

I got in trouble with her trying to explain how Fun scared me there in the boat. She kept asking why I was in the boat with that "fag" clown. There's lots of different kinds of scared, and I shouldn't of tried to explain it.

You might of read about this in the newspapers because it had all the stuff newspapers like. Sex, religion, tragedy, novelty aspects. I guess they were expecting a bunch of clowns to show up for the funeral, but we were all dressed in our Sunday best. The photographers didn't stick around. We were in disguise!

I've never met a retired clown, though I might be one myself pretty soon. I want to be a teacher now because that's a less reckless way of making a difference in the life of kids. I value life more because I saw somebody lose theirs and how fast that can happen.

I thought, a ride in a rowboat, what's the harm in it?

I'm glad I can rewrite this because I still don't think I figured out my conclusion yet. :) (Does this ever happen to you?) (I know I'm not supposed to use so many parenthesis, but that's how my mind works. Isn't that why they invented them in the first place?)

p.s. For my how-to paper, I want to write about Clown Survival in an Economic Downturn. Is that okay? I'm writing about what I know. . . . (I like those dotted lines.) You keep marking off for them, but they're legit punctuation, just like parenthesis. I'm exploring all my options here. I keep thinking about those dots like juggling balls. (I can juggle six, by the way. . . .)

HURTING A FLY

NOTHING EVER HAPPENED WHEN WE WENT AWAY, AND THAT WAS how my parents liked it. For many years, they were one unit, a plural singular in my daily life. I was the only "only child" on our street. I never wondered about my parents as separate people, never wondered why I was the only one, why they didn't trot out children year after year like all the other good Catholics on the block.

Neighbors took in our mail and newspapers, and my friend John B. took care of our dog, Snoopy. Nobody blinked when we left, and nobody blinked when we returned. "Snoopy"—that says it all, doesn't it? I'll take the blame for that. They got him for me—like everything else, a compensation. He slept at the foot of my bed every night and only bit somebody once.

Paul Binkowski, who deserved it, for more reasons than my parents ever knew.

I'm not sure why we even went away. Maybe simply because we could. With only one child, my parents could afford to take a vacation. The other kids stayed home. Oh, their fathers sometimes took a week off from the Ford plant, but nobody could afford to go anywhere with four, five, six kids.

Every summer we spent a week at Uncle Rob and Aunt Pearl's house in Keokuk, Iowa. Uncle Rob had gone to college. My dad always joked about Uncle Rob's job being to fire people, but Uncle Rob never laughed. I remember that because in our family, everybody was supposed to laugh at the same time. We were like a laugh track when we were together, synchronized and polite laughter at bad jokes about stinky dogs and pink elephants.

Even now, it's hard to imagine something happening while we were gone. If you walked down the street the day before we came home that year, you might not have noticed anything different about our three-bedroom ranch, identical to others on the street. We had a spare bedroom while everybody else was putting up plywood walls in their basements and shoving the kids down there.

Why did I start letting the boys touch me? I imagine some shrink could take me back and make me figure it all out, but maybe I don't want to know, or maybe I already do. I'm still spoiled, even at forty, my thighs chafing against each other in my jeans as I walk in the park under the theory that I might lose a few pounds, a theory my husband Bill is subtly encouraging. He got me a dog too, just the other day. I haven't even named it yet. It's the dog that's got me thinking. My husband doesn't know anything about those boys. We have no children.

When I told my parents I was pregnant, they began to split, like a tree struck by lightning, jagged edges sticking up, splintering the air. My father wanted to let me stay, to ride it out, but my mother wanted to send me away. Here I should be telling you what I wanted.

We drove to Ohio and got rid of it.

My parents had done that one scandalous thing—having me out of wedlock—then planned on packing it in for the rest of their lives. But I had more scandal inside me than both of them combined. I turned their hopes into scandal like wine into tainted water.

"Let her talk," my father said. My mother looked like she was going to rip the clothes off her own body. I would not talk.

I found Binkowski hanging out with his friends behind the bowling alley. That's where we used to meet, where we did what we did, against the wall, or lying in the weeds. He was one of many who marched back there with me. They were mostly from Dallas, an older street on the edge of our neighborhood. Less Polish, more Southern. Poorer and rougher. They all smoked, striking their boy poses.

John B. used to wait at the corner every day for the school bus to drop me off after kindergarten. He was only six months younger, but the way the birthdays broke down, he had to wait. We walked home together. We held hands.

When we came home and found Snoopy hanging from the clothesline pole in the yard, I screamed. Nobody screamed on our street, not like that. They yelled at their kids, they hollered at their spouses, but nobody screamed.

My father tackled me right before I reached Snoopy.

It seems like one of the hardest things in life is to know when to stop doing something you enjoy before you no longer enjoy it.

I immediately thought that Binkowski had done it, the casual cruelty that I knew firsthand. Something to make up for the humiliation of getting the fat girl pregnant.

The police arrived, sirens blazing. A strung-up dog. Not the usual vandalism or even a break-in. The firemen showed up too, and EMS—not for the dog, but for me. I wouldn't stop screaming. They strapped me down, shot me full of something to knock me out, and took me away. I remember the huge crowd stomping on our lawn, and my father screaming at everyone to get off his fucking grass. I'd never heard my father say *fuck* before, even when I told him I was pregnant.

A line had been crossed. It was like when Eddie Buck from over on Dallas shot Bill Stephens in the middle of a fistfight. Everybody got guns after that. Mr. Sunshine's Guns and TV Repair expanded, and Mr. Sunshine got himself the ugliest Cadillac known to man and drove it everywhere.

You don't just hang somebody's dog. The hospital kept me overnight, then my parents took me home, where all evidence of a hung dog had been dutifully removed. My mother had cut a small article out of the newspaper to hide it from me. The empty rectangle in the page freaked me out more than any article could have.

I remembered the neatly tied knot around Snoopy's neck. Not the kind of knot a hood like Binkowski would know a thing about.

"Tell 'em nothing," my father said. "We were out of town, and that's the truth." My parents had not mentioned my pregnancy to the police. A detective was coming to the house. My father was nervously biting his pipe stem, though the pipe was empty. He was puffing on nothing, making the *nothing* tangible.

They had told the police one thing: that John B. had been caring for the dog while we were gone, as he had always done. John B., who had nearly made Eagle Scout until he decided that Scouts were a bunch of phonies. It took him six years to figure that out, and it'd taken him two to figure out that the rumors about me were true. John B., a little slow on the uptake, a little heavy on the sincere loyalty, reliable as all those knots he learned in Scouts.

It'd be nice to tie this story together like one of those knots, but the rope is so frayed that I could pull it apart with one finger. John B. was one of eight kids and would never have his own dog. He loved that dog, but he killed it.

Cars crept by to look at the house where the dog got hung. Shame has an endless number of levels. I had gotten pregnant and had an abortion, and maybe more people knew about that than I had imagined, but everyone knew about the dog strung up on the laundry pole.

Phone off the hook, we crowded into the spare bedroom where we kept our TV. We sat in the dark with the set on, watching *whatever* in grim silence. It was like we ourselves were being hunted down.

I caught my father in the kitchen late that night throwing out the leftover dog food and the red plastic bowls, the leash. He looked up at me, then closed his eyes as if I was not there.

"Does this mean we're never getting another dog?" I asked.

"Never," he said. "Never again," he said, gently, as if it were a statement full of mercy and compassion.

John B.'s mother was the biggest anti-abortion lady on the street, a spokesperson for some radical Catholic group that papered the neighborhood with flyers. She went out of town to rallies.

John B. stayed in altar boys almost as long as Scouts. For a couple of years, he said he was going to be a priest. It seemed like he wanted me to talk him out of it, though I never even tried. "*Be* a priest," I'd tell him. Our neighborhood was mapped out like a rigged maze, with everybody ending up at the factory. I envied him the purity of his odd desire.

We had three other *Johns* on the block. Can you blame me for coming up with Snoopy?

I was always on the heavy side. My mother liked sweets too. She worked at a local bakery and brought home day-old doughnuts. I developed fast, and guess what? Boys noticed.

The neighborhood girls didn't like coming over to my house, where there were no other kids. They weren't used to the quiet, to having a parent like my mother nosing in and trying to supervise our games.

"John B.," I said. "Why'd you kill Snoopy?"

He tilted his head up and squinted, sitting on the one remaining saddle swing on the broken-down playground behind our old elementary school. They'd decided the paved surface was too dangerous after years and years of it being that way. The old stuff was rotting while they figured out what to do. I stood by a rusty metal pole, swinging in circles, my hand turning red with it. I'd always loved those saddle swings, leaning back until the world was all sky.

"How'd you figure that out?" he asked, sincere as ever.

"Knots," I said.

"Huh," he said.

"Why didn't you tell the police the truth?"

"Do you think it was easy, doing that to Snoop?" he asked. "I had to."

"Had to? Had to?" I shouted.

"I was gonna tell you. I heard what you done, and, well, this seemed right."

My head throbbed. I bent down to him on the swing. "What?" I spat in his face.

His face turned from a squint to a mask of anguish. "My mom," he said. He began to choke on his words. "Her way would've been to tell. My way is the secret way. God's secret way."

John B. and I had drifted into distant cousins, but we still were anchored together by all those years when he was my secret brother and I was—what was I for him? He could be a soft boy. We played with dolls and made fairy houses.

"God didn't have anything to do with it," I said. I hated him then. I dropped my hand hard onto his shoulder. "I know what I did, why wasn't that enough?"

"I wanted people to know," he said, "but then I got scared."

"You should've gotten scared sooner," I said.

"I wanted people to know *I* knew, see?" he said, as if he was a patient teacher, explaining an obvious answer.

They should've caught him, but John B. was a good liar for a Catholic boy. And I guess nearly everybody knew John B., and no one could say a bad thing about him, even the Scoutmaster who'd had his heart broken, losing his one shot at an Eagle Scout.

"He wouldn't hurt a fly," everybody said. "He loved that dog," they said. My parents said. I said.

Somewhere truth intersects with shame, and that's where God either comes in or takes a pass. He took a pass here. He was tired of our house, I think, and all the secret shames.

My mother wanted me to have an abortion because she didn't have that choice herself. She'd had me. I can't take that logic very far before it starts to smell like a dog hanging from a clothesline pole.

Snoopy looked nothing like the cartoon dog. I don't think a dog anywhere looks like that. Every year when we got home from vacation, John B. used to make the same joke about Snoopy never crapping in the cartoons.

"Nobody craps in cartoons," I'd tell him. I never took much stock in cartoons myself. I guess Snoopy was the only dog name I knew. Who knows what a little girl like that is thinking, a little girl who could do no wrong.

John B. cleaned up the crap in that yard better than I ever did, every single bit of it. My only chore, and my father covered for me half the time. Nobody played in our yard. It just accumulated back there.

Oh, John B., my darling stupid boy.

We moved away the next spring. My father was a go-along-to-get-along guy, but he finally agreed there was no more getting along for us there where Snoopy was hung and his daughter had gotten pregnant.

We never went to visit my uncle who fired people again. We invited them to visit us, but they never came. The mailman forwarded our mail for about a year, then it stopped coming. Nothing for me.

I was sixteen and really didn't care about Snoopy anymore. He was old. I hated staying home in that silent house. When I'd go out, he'd stand at the door with my sad parents as if I was betraying them all.

If you've got shame and the truth, then cruelty should be in there too. Cruelty, to smudge all the intersecting lines so that even God turns his back.

"It was a boy who hung Snoopy," my father said years later, half statement, half question. "But was it that one?"

"Dad, it was all of them," I said.

JOYRIDE

Snow, with more snow coming. It buried the road in one endless tidal wave, no moon to pull it back.

Ronnie Barker—Bark, his friends called him—had stolen a rusty black Ford station wagon out of the Farmer Jack's parking lot. Old cars were easiest to steal. Almost too easy. Barker was hoping he'd be able to drop that from his repertoire of crimes soon, maybe grow up some and get a job or some wacky shit like that. He'd be out of school in four months, with or without a diploma, depending on who he could casually intimidate to help him cheat on his finals.

Intimidation could be subtle, Bark realized during his stint in the Navy sponsored by a local judge who'd offered jail as the alternative. He simply needed to scope out each class and politely ask the smallest, smartest kid for the answers. Bark was six foot four, 250—a nice chunk of change. While his Navy muscles had lost some of their tone, he still had enough to scare the little shits. That, and his reputation.

His friends had piled in when he'd pulled up behind the high school, where they were huddled like raggedy robins who'd forgotten to check out for winter, missing the bus south, and nothing to do about it but pass around a couple of joints in the cold and blow on their hands as if stoking their own heartbeats. If he hadn't stolen the car, Barker would've been out there with them, like the guys who hung outside the temp agency every morning hoping to pick up some work. That's where Bark would have to start looking for a job—that, or fast food, but temp work paid better when work was to be had. Or, a life of crime. Whatever happened, Bark couldn't go back in the Navy. They'd seen enough of his stubborn, sorry self. If he got in trouble again, it'd be jail for sure. "Life of crime, life of time," he mumbled to himself as if it were the disembodied refrain of some heavy metal song. It clashed against whatever blared from the radio—bad music turned up loud.

He counted in the rearview mirror—four of them back there. Heater was rocking out the BTUs. Body rusting out, but nothing wrong with the heater. "What the fuck's a BTU?" Barker shouted above the radio—no tapes, CDs, or nothing. Must be some old-dude car. He could turn it down, but what was the point. No one answered. Perhaps no one heard him. Someone shouted, "Fuck you too." Maybe that was his answer.

Still and rigid as a thin nail next to him in the middle of the seat sat Jeanine, who was under orders never to see him again. But when he'd swung the car around, she'd landed right up front in her old spot. Jeanine wasn't kicking out the BTUs. She was shivering. Bark put his hand around her skinny thigh and rubbed up and down her jeans.

"Good heater in here," he said.

"I can't hear either," she said, and he turned down the music.

"I've been missing you," he said, and everybody heard.

"Where we off to, Captain Barker?" It was Tater, once everyone's favorite catcher, and now nobody's favorite friend. Tater had stopped playing baseball and had stopped being of use to them as a buyer too. Once Barker came back from the Navy, he was more than happy to buy everybody's booze. Tater had joined them in eighth grade as a sixteen-year-old from Kentucky. Once the baseball league discovered how old he really was—it took years for that birth certificate from Kentucky to materialize—it didn't matter how old he was for baseball. He was old enough to buy booze, and that had counted more than hitting taters. But when Barker returned, old Tater was just another fat guy who laughed too loud and got on everybody's nerves.

"My grandfather's cottage," Barker shouted. Everyone quieted down. The heater blower hissed and huffed.

"Where the hell's that?" Vickie asked. Vickie, the shy, sullen one Jeanine confided in.

"We didn't even know you had a grandfather," Ken said. "We thought you'd emerged on the scene fully formed, tattoos and all." Barker imagined Ken in the backseat, winking at someone.

Barker worried about becoming the new Tater. Why did these kids hang around with him? Two years in the Navy. Nobody ever asked him about it. He'd been in school with some of their older brothers and sisters. What was he doing back in high school? It was like a board game where you pretended to be somebody else, to care about things you did not care about. To use play money.

"Yeah, we thought you were an alien, dude. Arriving in this spaceship from planet Fuck-you-up," Kimmy O. said, the smart mouth, the wicked angry girl everyone was half afraid of.

"Farmer Jack's, man. Planet Farmer Jack's," Barker said, hoping to get a laugh.

"Hey, I think this is *my* car," Ken shouted. "I think I did Kimmy O. on this seat back here. Remember, Kimmy?"

Kimmy smacked him, the others howled, and everybody forgot about his grandfather's cottage except Jeanine, who tugged on his jacket sleeve as if he was working the checkout at Farmer Jack's and forgot to give her change. She wanted her change.

"You wish," Kimmy O. said, just to clarify.

"Take me home, Ron," Jeanine whispered. "It won't be worth it."

The wipers waved at the snow, and the snow dodged them, overwhelmed them.

"It might be," he said. "If we could get rid of everybody else."

"Where were you planning on going when you found us?"

"My grandpa's cottage, like I said."

"By yourself?"

"He's dying, okay? Just want to go up there and smell the place." He knew that sounded strange. "Something like that," he added softly.

Ron Barker—half a dozen Warren cops knew him by name, slowed down next to him while he walked down the street. Waved. Beeped their horn. Pulled him over and patted him down if they were bored. Make the big guy squirm—a good game for slow nights in the city. They pulled rank on him. He had no rank, just a big Navy lunkhead back in high school. Get a job, they told him.

Officer McDonald called him Chief Barking-Up-the-Wrong-Tree—said it was his Indian name. There weren't any Indians in Warren, Michigan. Just cowboys holding pissing contests on street corners and parking lots until they got bored enough to break something or to break into something, both illegal under local statutes.

The charge that sent him out to sea involved some version of a Molotov cocktail Barker had put together and thrown through the window of Platski's Drugs, a drug store/package liquor store that had been selling to Bark since age fifteen, but then suddenly refused his fake ID when he had a car full of friends waiting. The cocktail did not ignite, but Mr. Platski did.

"With all due respect, Mr. Caruso, fuck you." Bark had meant to say, "I love your daughter, and no way can you keep us apart," but it came out wrong. He had the bad habit of sprinkling *fucks* into his everyday conversation like sugar on donuts. The assistant principal, Mr. Walker, an old Navy man himself, just shook his head at the little detention slips in Barker's enormous hands. He barely fit in the desks, his thick legs turned sideways, tripping everyone who passed, everyone who had hoped he was gone but now he was back.

Mr. Walker had become a semi-friend of the Barker family, particularly Mrs. Barker—Helen—who, through their frequent meetings before Barker entered the Navy, had taken a shine to him. Sometimes Barker wondered if the only reason his mother was making him finish high school was to get reacquainted with Mr. Walker.

Mr. Caruso, like Jeanine, was a wisp. Thin in a coat-hanger kind of way—gnarled, tight, hollow, and pissed off. He worked at Chrysler driving a hi-lo. He was sensitive about his height, Jeanine said. He combed his hair back like a greaser and strutted like a broken toy.

Jeanine carried her passion tightly wrapped around her tiny bones. It rarely emerged, but sometimes, when they were parked on the dead end of Keller Court in whatever random vehicle Bark had come up with, it felt like she was kicking his ass when they made love, her bones banging against his, her angles thrusting against him in jumbled ecstasy. She wanted to be filled with something he could not give her. Not even him, the one guy in the neighborhood who had been outside the country, who had seen something—even if he had not been paying attention and was now back cruising the old streets, two years older, enjoying the ride through one last year of high school in order to please his mother, who *seriously* could kick anyone's ass. Who'd sent her first husband packing, limping from a kick to the balls, according to his dying grandfather, dying because he simply could not stop smoking.

They had arrived at Jeanine's house near dawn, the sky graying above the tiny box houses of Warren. Jeanine had not wanted to go home. Sure, earlier that night they'd steamed up the windows of the stolen car—a big Mercury—but at the Red Apple, a twenty-four-hour diner next to the Salvation Army on Nine Mile Road, they'd spent hours just talking about sober dreams. Jeanine's dreams all had to do with getting away. Barker loved watching her face flush, her tiny hands curling into fists as she imagined a future that included him.

Mr. Caruso had been up all night waiting, jazzed on coffee or speed or pure rage. He stood in the driveway, caught in the headlights of the stolen car. "You will never see my daughter again," he'd said, trying to get up in Barker's face as if he'd been rehearsing it. But he only came up to Bark's neck. His breath stunk, Barker remembered. He'd never liked Barker taking Jeanine out. He called Bark "the criminal," Jeanine told him.

"Dad," Jeanine said, and he'd pushed her away, then stepped into Barker and shoved him against the bricks of the house next door. Bark peeled away Jeanine, who had run back between them, and charged at Mr. Caruso.

He hadn't meant to punch him, but that sort of went the way of the tactful language. Just two punches, but the little man reeled and fell into the bricks of his own house, then slumped down.

For a moment, it looked like she was going to leave with him, but lights were coming on in the houses around them. "Get out of here, Bark," Jeanine shouted. She ran into her house, a horse running back into a barn during a fire. He drove off in the Mercury, then ditched it in the parking lot at the Ford Plant over on Mound Road and walked home, cursing himself, knowing he'd done something he couldn't take back, that he'd booby-trapped his own life yet again.

Now, a month later, Jeanine was next to him again. Her father couldn't keep them from seeing each other at school, though they shared none of the same classes. She was college prep, and he was vo-tech. Aside from brief minutes in the hallways at school, this was the first time since then that they were together.

The snow bounced off the car and slid parallel to the ground before landing behind them, accumulating. It took an hour to drive to the cottage in the best of weather. "The driver needs a drink," Barker said, and somebody passed forward a pint of peppermint schnapps. He took a swallow and gritted his teeth. He hated that sweet shit, but somebody back there liked it.

"This is stupid," Tater said. "What are we gonna do up at this cottage except freeze our asses off?"

"Build a fire. Toast our toes," Barker said cheerfully.

"Create friction," Kimmy O. said.

"We already got friction," Tater said.

"Smooth friction. They got beds in that cottage, right Bark?" That was Ken. Somebody'd get into a bed with Ken—that could be counted on. The handsome one who could talk his way into and out of anything. Barker admired and hated him.

"Is this snow fucked up, or what?" Kimmy said, her voice edged with worry.

"We got beds," Barker said. "Me and my brothers used to come up here on weekends. My grandpa put warm bricks in our beds to keep us toasty."

Barker knew that none of them could stay out all night without consequences. He felt his power over them now—the power to instill fear. They'd left the safety of their familiar streets, where they could opt out, get dropped off on a random corner and walk home. They were stuck with Barker in a stolen car in a snowstorm. His own parents didn't care where he was as long as it wasn't jail.

"Warm bricks? Shit, I'm talking about love, I'm talking romance, I'm talking spiritual oneness, and he's talking warm bricks. I'll take two girls in my bed, and we'll leave Bark with the warm bricks," Ken said. They all laughed nervously, except Jeanine, who sat paralyzed, staring out the window.

"Bark, did you really kick her dad's ass?" Tater asked.

Bark sighed. "I didn't kick nobody's ass. Little guy was rightly pissed off at me for keeping his daughter out all night." Bark glanced at Jeanine. "Didn't mean to hurt him. Not at all." The car fishtailed a bit, but Barker straightened it out. "His feelings were hurt is all."

He looked over at Jeanine. She was biting her lip. He knew these clowns—her friends, mostly—must have asked her the same thing. He wondered what she'd told them.

"He didn't have me busted, and I'm mighty glad of that."

Barker knew Jeanine blamed him. His banishment made everything more difficult—impossible. Yet here they were. If they were going to risk being together, at least make it worth the risk, he could hear her thinking, not just joyriding through a blizzard, joyless and not alone.

"Jeanine and I are getting married," he said.

Jeanine closed her eyes. Barker was having trouble seeing the road through the layers of snow, the tires fishtailing again as he changed lanes on I-94. He wished he'd taken a look at the tires.

Barker turned the key and put his shoulder to the door. It quickly swung open, snow angling in onto the old linoleum. A sleeping bag and blankets lay bunched up on the couch, and half a loaf of bread and a jar of grape jelly sat on his grandmother's sticky oilcloth on the room's one table. She'd died while Barker was in the Navy, and he'd gotten a leave to return for the funeral, though he spent the whole time drunk.

A few bricks sat on top of the cold oil heater.

"Looks like somebody's living here," Jeanine whispered.

"Well, it sure ain't my grandpa," Barker said. He guessed it was his Uncle Right John. He hoped his father was behind this, a little secret between the two of them. But where was his uncle now, in this blizzard?

Barker found a pile of burned matches near the pilot light. He thought maybe it was out of oil, but the burner quickly lit. Maybe his uncle had been unable to remember how to light it, or was simply too drunk to accomplish the task. Maybe he was keeping the heater off while he was gone to conserve oil. Maybe nobody knew he was here.

Barker peered through a dusty window at the outhouse. The door swung open in the wind.

"It'll heat up," Barker assured the shivering group huddled around him.

"This ain't gonna be like one of those horror movies, is it?" Tater asked. "Where the psycho guy comes back and terrorizes the teenagers?" Nobody laughed.

"If anyone comes in, it'll be my Uncle Right John, and all he'll do is drink whatever booze you've got left. He's a terror when it comes to booze."

"Bark is the psycho guy, but we're his friends, so we're safe, right Bark?" Ken said.

"Shut up, Ken," Barker said. Why had he picked them all up? Had he even asked them, or had they simply piled in? Sometimes he just didn't think. Would they be able to get back to the main road through the deep snow? Was his uncle freezing to death out there somewhere?

He turned on his grandfather's radio with the big light-up dial and tuned in a crackly oldies station. "Jeanine and I are going to rest awhile in this bedroom," Barker said. "Anyone is welcome to use the other one," he added. He looked around at the others. "Well, party on," he said, leading Jeanine behind the dingy curtain his grandfather had hung instead of a door.

The bare studs were visible, the rooms unfinished forever. Every sound in the tiny cottage was audible, every breath. The silver backing of the insulation reflected the dim light bulb before Barker clicked it off. He and Jeanine climbed into the bed and threw themselves against each other. Barker felt her mouth press into him so hard it hurt, and he briefly pulled back.

In each other's arms, they forgot that they were not alone in the tiny cottage—shack, really. His barracks in the Navy were luxurious compared to this, but the memories of his grandfather's gruff kindness here made Barker feel safer than just about anywhere.

"Okay, big boy, let's do it," Jeanine said, wrapping her thin arms around his thick chest. She seemed relaxed, content, even confident. Sexual release maybe, but something else too.

"We just did it, Sweetie," Barker said. He didn't want to make the drive back tonight, but he had to. Her father said he'd press charges if anything else happened.

"I mean get married."

"Sure, babe, we can get married." Her long hair tickled his bare chest. He pulled up the musty old quilt over her shoulder.

"Hey, Bark, what about those warm bricks you were getting all weepy about?" Ken shouted from the other bedroom, though he sounded like he was standing at the foot of their bed. The snow pushing in on all sides seemed to amplify the tiny square space of the cottage.

"They're right on top of the heater," Bark said. He thought of his grandfather in the hospital wheezing with emphysema, the stink of the room, his pale thin body like smoke ready to dissipate forever.

He knew something was wrong with Uncle Right John—he hadn't been to the hospital to visit his own father. Maybe his body was buried in this blizzard.

"I mean now," Jeanine whispered.

Bark laughed nervously. He got up and pulled the chain on the ceiling bulb. They could see their breath in the dim light. "But, Babe, we need money for that. . . . Why do you think I steal cars?" He began getting dressed. "I slept in a room full of other guys for two years. I'm happy being home again." Bark surprised himself—he thought he sounded wimpy.

"I'm not," she said. "Fuck college, by the way," she said, apropos of nothing.

"College is good," he said. "Not for me," he said quickly, "for you. No jobs here. Everybody getting laid off. My old man's bringing home bomb pops for dinner. Bullshit and bomb pops. . . . We gotta get you home," he said suddenly.

"I'm tired of hanging out in parking lots," she said.

"Everybody get dressed. Or whatever," he shouted.

Outside, snow had covered all their tracks. He held his grandfather's key in his fist, the key his grandfather had secretly handed him in the hospital last week, asking him to check on the place. Some day the cottage might be his, if his father found a way to keep paying the taxes. Or else his uncle would burn it down trying to keep warm. They called him Right John because John was boring, and he was always saying, "Right," though he never listened to anyone.

Bark pushed the curtain aside. Tater and Vickie sat glum on the couch. Uncle Right John's pile of sour bedding had been tossed into a corner. Either something had happened between them, or nothing. Ken and Kimmy emerged from behind the other curtain like a couple of shy actors stepping on stage. They were holding hands. Barker grabbed Jeanine's hand.

"Let's see if we can get out of here," Barker said. He hesitated at the door. Maybe his uncle has lost his key. The cottage was locked when they'd arrived. Bark left it unlocked.

The girls took turns in the outhouse, screaming with the cold on their bare skin while the boys pissed in the snow. The car started right up, and Barker cranked the heater full blast.

The car quickly became stuck in a snow-covered ditch. Jeanine steered while the rest of them leaned against the trunk, slipping, cursing, till the car gained traction on the packed snow of the empty road. Barker took the wheel and followed the wide tracks a truck had made. They slid off the road two more times before finally reaching the interstate.

"Who's going to help me with the Michigan history final?" he asked in the silent car as it crawled back down the freeway. The plows had already hit it once or twice, but the snow was relentless.

Nobody answered. Nobody missed him when he was in the Navy. Nobody'd miss him if he left again. He was a novelty act, good for maybe one year. He was sure Tater could tell him all about it.

"Just get us home, big boy," Ken finally said.

"Chicken," Jeanine whispered. "If you loved me, you'd find a way." She pounded on his knee with her tiny, gloved fist.

Did she love him or the *idea* of him? He was still astounded by her stubborn attachment to him in the face of her mad father. Bark had ruined her reputation. What did she see in him? Nobody was going to help him study on that.

"What if I was pregnant?" she asked, not bothering to whisper. He held the wheel steady. He slowed down and dragged his foot to make sure he was still on the road.

"That'd be no good," he said soberly. He knew guys in the Navy who'd gotten their girlfriends pregnant and had been forced into marriage. Get somebody pregnant, join the Navy. Get busted, join the Navy. Bomb pops and bullshit.

"Why would you want to marry me?" Barker felt his slack belly pressing tight against his belt. Muscle—the one thing the Navy had given him, and he was losing it.

"You kicked my father's ass," she said, and she said no more.

"See, I told you," he heard Tater mumble.

The clock in the car was broken. Bark never wore a watch. After all the attention to time in the military, he'd been careless with it, he realized now, thinking it was unlimited.

"What'd your father ever do to you?" Barker asked. He leaned his ear against the cold window.

The car edged along the freeway in a long line of headlights obscured by snow. In ditches on either side, cars had helplessly slid and sat abandoned for the night. He was grateful for the weight of the others in the back giving him traction. He'd also thrown a few bricks in the trunk. The next time he looked over at Jeanine, tears were streaking her cheeks, and he knew she had not told him everything.

Back on the flat streets of Warren, Barker drove more aggressively, swerving around icy corners as he dropped the others off one by one. Nobody said thanks or see you later. Barker's mouth was dry and sour. He half wanted a swig of peppermint schnapps, but it was long gone.

Jeanine was last. She had him stop around the corner from her house.

"If he ever touched you, I'll kill him now," Barker said flatly.

She slipped off a glove and put her small finger against his lips.

"Do something *good* crazy," she said. "Surprise everyone. Marry me. Let's make a plan. I need a plan to live on."

"I'm no good on planning. You make us a plan, and I'll sign onto it," he said. He ached for her. He knew it was dangerous to want one thing, just one thing, so much. His grandfather was checking out, and Uncle Right John could be just about anywhere, alive or dead.

"I will." She smiled, kissed him, and got out of the car, struggling through the deep snow. He sat idling at the corner till she got inside and turned off the porch light. He wanted to write something in ink, not just the same sweaty pencils they used for tests at school. Fill in the circle completely. That was hard enough, even if he knew the answer.

He pulled into the empty Farmer Jack's parking lot under the passive floodlights, the snow angling across them like mad stars. He was sorry to give up the car now—it was just starting to feel right. A snowplow was crossing back and forth, heaving large piles of snow into mountains, clearing things out for the morning. A thin layer of packed snow covered where the plow had driven. They'd salt that later—bring back the slanted yellow lines marking out the spaces. He gunned the engine, yanked the wheel, and spun a series of donuts over the smooth surface. The plow driver idled, watching. The car came to rest where it had started.

Barker got out and waved to the plow driver, then began trudging home. The snow was drifting high against fences and buildings and parked cars. It'd take everyone a long time to dig out from the storm. He himself was in no hurry.

HELD BACK

Somebody dies at the end. Somebody always dies at the end. It's like you've got a couple of pens—exactly the same pens—and then you lose the top to one of them. A felt pen, so it's going to dry out if you don't find that other top. But you never do, and for the rest of your life you're wondering, maybe I should've switched the top from the other pen to that one. Maybe it had more juice left.

Or maybe it's not like that at all. My life has sped away from her death like an arrow with a thin line of razor wire attached—almost invisible, but try and walk through it, it'll cut your head off.

She was beautiful and young, and she died at age twenty-two. She would've been twenty-three in July, but she died in late December, in the middle of her senior year. Slim, I called her. Her name was Kim Salvia. She'd been held back in first grade because the teacher thought her too dreamy. Not many people at Alba knew that—Alba College. I was a senior too, and more than half in love with Slim. She stood six-foot one with long, sway-ing blonde hair. She never had the slouch of some tall girls. If anything, her body appeared to be reaching upward, straining to extend itself further into the world. When she tilted her head to listen to me, her hair hung straight like a glistening curtain, and I wanted to kiss her secret, exposed ear. Some-times I did.

My friend Charles had driven up from Detroit because his fiancée, Robin, had just dumped him. We'd already gotten measured for our tuxes, so it was serious shit, and he wanted to get away, visit me, his old pal LC—Lawrence Carter, his running buddy from back home who'd gone off to college to seek his fortune, and thus was constantly mooching money every time he came home and wanting to stay out all night, even when all the other homeboys had to get up and punch in at the factory the next day.

Kim was driving back to Detroit—passing Charles on I-96 driving the other way, most likely—to see Robert Fripp at Ford Auditorium. Robert fucking Fripp. She was into that weird King Crimson shit. That was the thing with her—she *was* dreamy. It took us three years to fall in love with each other because she sway-danced like a hippie, and I danced like a rocker when I danced at all—all stomp, no flow. We fell into each other's arms the minute we returned to campus that fall, and all she did was hug me one millisecond longer than usual, but it was long enough for me to know that was where I wanted to be.

So, what was I doing sleeping with Gina? Yeah, somebody cheats on somebody, that's part of it too. While Kim was out of town, LC (me again) got really drunk and slept with Gina, one of Kim's friends—though I was wildly incapable of finishing what I started, so technically the act was not consummated. Until the following morning. This is a confession, so I guess God's in the house too.

I didn't know what to do with Charles, or what he was expecting, but after I let him in, he pulled out a fifth of whiskey and his hash pipe, and we didn't say much, sitting at the old sticky kitchen table in the house I shared with some hippies who were trying to smooth out my rough edges and get me to *just mellow out.* They were friends of Kim's, which is how we met, though Alba was so small, you met everyone eventually, whether you wanted to or not.

Charles kept trying to give me money back for my lost deposit on the tux, but I kept waving him off in some odd ritual of affection. It was the only thing I could think to offer, some small monetary consolation. Words weren't doing much good. After we killed the whiskey, we took to the streets to walk my dog, Mudboy. I saw the light on at Gina's. She and I had slept together the previous year, and we were part of the same weird circle of friends who had, it seemed, all slept with each other at some point and gotten it over with, though sometimes paired up again in one random configuration or another.

"Larry—hey what's up?" Gina said. Nobody at school knew a guy named LC. She yanked her door open like she herself was making a grand entrance.

"My friend Charles," I gestured to him, "up from Detroit. We're partying."

"I see you brought *another* friend," Gina said. "Oh, Mudboy, how you doing, you big baby."

She bent down to pet Mudboy, a black lab with a bit too much spirit. A dog I had gotten maybe because "chicks dig dogs" or because my girlfriend from freshman year, Cathy with a C, had moved in across the street from me with Michael, the wimpy little painter with the curly hair who *just understood everything* in ways I was apparently incapable of.

"You're looking kind of wasted." Gina grabbed me around the waist and pulled me into her apartment, Charles staggering in behind us. I dropped Mudboy's leash, and he started roaming around, whacking everything with his big tail and snorfling a pile of Gina's clothes in the corner.

"Chill out, Mudboy," I said. I kicked the snow off my boots and then fell back into the pile of clothes. It had started to snow as soon as Charles arrived, and it was still coming down hard. Kim loved snow, and if she were there, we'd have been out rolling around in it and laughing. I was already ashamed in advance of where I knew the night would take us.

"Have a seat, Charles," we both said at the same time, though there were no seats, and I'd already claimed the clothes pile. Charles had drunk his way up the interstate, so he'd had a head start that was catching up with him.

"What's new in Detroit?" Gina asked.

Charles tried to speak. It sounded like "Bleaay, bleeah, yeck." Then he broke into tears, his head sinking down into his thick neck as he tilted over onto the ratty green rug.

"His financier dumped him right before the wedding," I said, rolling my eyes for only Gina to see, because at college marriage was frowned upon as some ridiculous setup that had produced our dull parents. She let the financier/fiancée thing slide. It wasn't a term we threw around much.

"Bummer," she said. "What's a young stud like you wanting to get married for anyway? Aren't you in college somewhere?"

None of my friends back home were in college. Gina would've known that if we'd ever actually had a serious conversation about anything. Mostly, we just got stoned and had sex, though that had stopped since things with Kim had taken a serious turn. Gina was my first after old whatshername living across the street with wimpy whatshisname.

Charles had calmed down a bit, but he could only shake his head. He was working afternoon shift at Chrysler's, which might have given Robin some time for bobbin' with somebody else. She'd told him that wasn't true, but they always say that. I've said it myself. Unless you're actually caught in the act, why hurt someone even worse? I preferred to be lied to.

You know how sometimes the weather's in this in-between place and you keep taking off your jacket then putting it on again, then you end up leaving it in somebody's car, or worse, back at the bar where you'll never see it again? Gina and I were like that. Some good things there—random, unpredictable sparks—but not anything we'd write home about if we ever wrote home. Maybe she would've given Charles a tumble if he weren't so drunk and lovesick, if he hadn't fallen asleep on her floor. Mudboy kept licking his face, which made him laugh in his sleep, and I took that as a good sign.

Charles finally got up and agreed to walk Mudboy back to my place, where he fell asleep in his clothes on the dog-hair-covered couch. I found him there the next morning, along with Mudboy, who was stupidly wagging his tail, happy to see me when I returned from Gina's.

See what I mean? I was disloyal to my girlfriend, my best friend, and my dog, all in one night—the trifecta of bad behavior.

"I don't know, Larry. What about Kim? She's my friend—I don't want . . ." She was pulling my shirt off as she talked.

"We don't have one of those—whachacallit—agreements of exclusivelessness. She's down there with Robert fucking Tripp right now."

"Fripp. It's Fripp. And she's not sleeping with him."

"But would she if she could?"

"Larry."

"Did I ever tell you I like your underwear, how it's shiny and smooth and everything?"

"It's okay—I'm too wasted," I said after various manipulations and manifestations. It had become obvious at that point. Then I fell asleep and in the morning woke her up with hungover hard-on urgency.

"That's the Larry I know." Gina laughed sleepily and pulled me to her. She was a sociology major from New York who talked about "the city" and dressed up like Lou Reed for Halloween. She was no Kim. I would have grown up for Kim. I could have even grown to appreciate King Crimson, given the time, but at that age, time was a coupon with no expiration date. It always gave me a discount, it never turned, went bad.

Out on Old U.S. 27, between Elwell and Shepherd, a pipe stuck out of the ground, and anyone could drive up and fill up jugs full of cold, wonderful spring water. That fall, when we'd first started going out, Slim and I drove there in my old Plymouth, skidding to a stop in the gravel at the side of the road. We jerked forward, then back, in sync, laughing as empty plastic milk jugs tumbled over us from the backseat.

They just stuck "Old" in front of the road instead of renaming it. Old Slim and Old LC on Old 27. In three months, she'd be twenty-two forever. *Melodrama,* she'd say to that. And I'd say, *I'm no stranger to Melodrama. In fact, I've slept with Melodrama,* and she'd hit me over the head with one of those jugs.

We tossed the empty jugs into the weeds, and she did a little dance around the pipe. The kind of dance one does when surrounded by fields of flatness to rise above the earth, to levitate.

"C'mon, tough guy," Slim said. "Let's boogie." I just smiled. I felt exposed on Old 27, the cars and trucks whizzing past on that long straight road, though whatever held me back was breaking down bit by bit under your gentle prodding, and I like to imagine, given enough time with you, I might have even stripped naked and danced down the yellow line in the middle of the road.

There I go, switching to you again. That happens a lot when people die. I want to go on talking to them, reminding them of that one time when. . . . Fair doesn't have anything to do with it. I've been trying to write about her for twenty-eight years and counting, passing right on by Old 27—all I got so far is "Her hair like lit candles and a voice far off singing." Or "She is the one pipe sticking above the earth, the one that flows always."

The world was no trick when water tasting like earth itself came out of a pipe in the Middle of the Mitten, where Old U.S. 27 and U.S. 46 cut the lower Peninsula into four quadrants, where each winter the snow belt blew across in a band as wide as the gap between two horizontal lines of that giant palm.

We filled the jugs one by one and shoved them into the back of the car, till driving home I could not see behind me. On the way, we stopped at the Elwell Tavern, where we met two aging former Edmore Potato Festival Queens.

"How lucky is this?" Slim asked.

"Pretty damn," I said. "French fries for everyone."

She fed me french fries and licked the ketchup off my face as the setting sun shone through the bar's ancient glass-block windows.

I'm not too crazy about still being sad. Just a little crazy. The Plymouth— it was a Satellite—was so loaded down with spring water that it scraped bottom backing up onto the road. Kim made up a song about jugs in space that would bear repeating if I could remember it. Or maybe it was all in the presentation.

After she died, I shared the last of the water with Mudboy, pouring some into his red plastic bowl. A gesture I believe she'd have appreciated, she who loved dogs and children and—

It's winter now, like when she died. Her nose would be running if she were here, pushing fifty, like me. Excuse me for believing she'd still be lighting up the world—

Let me throw it in reverse, though I can't see out the back window: her long blonde hair hanging sideways from her tilted head as she bent toward the pipe, her throat opened to the cold, cold earth-water. Her breasts hung loose under her peasant blouse, sweat trickling down between them. I was going to say something smart about that, but I just watched her neck as she swallowed. The most beautiful thing I'd ever seen: a neck swallowing water. Who could've predicted that?

When she'd had enough, she looked at me, a little trickle at the side of her mouth, and she smiled. Then we lived happily ever after. . . .

"Charles, man, I'm sorry I kinda blew you off last night."

"What am I gonna do, LC?"

"Let's smoke a bowl, drink some coffee, and eat some weighty pancakes."

"After that."

"You drive back home and tell Robin to fuck off."

"Is that what you told Cathy?"

"Nah, I broke down and cried. I got down on my knees in the middle of the street in front of her house and begged her to come back. But that's just me."

"I don't get it. It's like being by herself is better than being with me."

"Sure she ain't got something on the back burner? Something cooking on the side? Somebody knocking on the back door? Somebody driving slow by her house, honking then speeding off?"

"What?" He shook his head. "Not Robin. You forget what it's like back home. I've been over her house every night planning the fucking wedding, then yesterday she says, 'No wedding. I need time to think.' I says, 'Does that mean we're still engaged while you're thinking?' Then she doesn't say anything, she just takes the ring off and . . .'"

Charles pulled the ring out of his pocket for the hundredth time since he showed up and started to cry again. "Who needs time to think?" he murmured. "Thinking, man, it just don't pay. Everybody knows that."

"There's a guy up here who hugs trees," I said, hoping to change the subject. I knew Robin did indeed have someone else, having heard it from my brother on the phone right before Charles showed up.

"See, that's it. Fucker's got too much time to think."

"He got up in English class when we were reading some poetry—Walt Whitman, by the way, who seems like kind of an asshole, but once in a while I think he's onto something—he gets up and says, 'I dig this Whitman dude. *I* hug trees.'"

"We all laughed. Even Miss Mousy, the politest girl in the world from St. Louis, Michigan, the 'official' Middle of the Mitten, gives a little titter. Then a couple weeks later, I see him down by the river actually *hugging* tree after tree."

"How much is this college shit costing you again?" Charles scratched his unshaven chin.

"Mudboy ran up to him, sniffing around like he was gonna piss on him, but then the guy sees me and starts waving like I'm a hundred miles away, though I'm only about maybe thirty yards. 'Want to hug trees with me?' he asks."

"Dude must be lonely or crazy."

"Lonely, that's what Kim said."

"What'd you say?"

"'Nah.' I just said, 'Nah.'"

"You ain't told me much about Kim," he says. "What was that all about last night?"

I was starting to feel hungover with what I'd done. "Kim's cool," I said. "You'll meet her." Though he never did.

Kim. Slim Kim. We had taken our sleeping bags down to the river to sleep under the stars on the clearest night in the history of the world, Alba, Michigan, version. We lay on the banks of the Pine River. She was writing a song in pencil in her tiny blue notebook, trying to come up with a good rhyme for "fear."

"Beer," I whispered, and she hit me. Our sleeping bags, though two different brands, two different colors—red and blue—magically zipped together, and we lay curled into each other for warmth. I was exactly her height. She was so thin that she chilled easily, her lips bluing, even through her smiling, chattering teeth. Mid-October—a little late for sleeping out in mid-Michigan. But the sky was clear, the moon was a whopper, and the river electric with flashes of white foam and glints of light.

"Atmosphere," she said, writing it down.

"There's a lot of rhymes with that 'ear' sound," I said, listing them alphabetically in my head. "I am mere without you near," I said and kissed her on the ear. "Ear," I whispered.

She reached around and pulled me tighter into her.

"Walt Whitman didn't use rhymes."

"That's what makes him cool," she said. Kim was a literature and art double major. She was going into elementary education. I was majoring in business. My father insisted that I study something that could make me his boss one day.

I have no idea why Kim fell in love with me. Maybe it was what she called karma. She had gone to Warren Woods High School, and I had gone to Warren Fitzgerald. We were the only two kids from the city of Warren—a suburb full of factories on the edge of Detroit—in the whole college of twelve hundred. If kids from Warren went anywhere, it was to community college or Wayne State. In the rare case of going away, they went to Michigan State. Nobody in Warren had even heard of Alba, but both Kim and I had found it. Both of us needed that middle-of-nowhere in order to find ourselves. I wanted to stop drinking and dry out (that part didn't work out so well), and I didn't want to follow the boys into the factory, so a small college hours away seemed like the perfect place to sober up and hide out. I think Kim needed to go to a place where they didn't think she was too dreamy. Where they didn't expect her to play basketball. Where they didn't expect her to have the baby if she got pregnant. Where it was okay to hug trees (even if they laughed at you).

I would have hugged trees for her, that's what I'm trying to say. Because she wasn't crazy or lonely. Open, that's the word. She had these long arms, and when she spread them to take me in, I felt like the world had granted me some special privilege.

We had three months. Could it have been real, lasting love, given enough time? Time, time—that was the rhyme that killed her.

"Psst. There's the tree guy," I whispered. We watched in silence as he moved through the woods hugging trees. Not every tree. He had some kind of system—I could never get far enough into the head of somebody like that to figure out what it might be.

"He must be lonely," Slim said. She snuggled down, putting her ear next to the ground as if maybe she could hear his soul sliding through the dying grass. Mudboy ran up to Tree Hug and nosed him in the crotch, but he just bent down and petted the dog—said some words and scratched his ear. Mudboy followed him for a distance, then returned to our little campsite.

I liked calling her Slim because of the liquid sounds that mimicked her flow through life. She didn't have a hard *K* in her body.

"Maybe you're right," I said. "That bark must be rough." I put my ear to her back.

"As rough as your beard," she laughed. Mudboy curled up on top of our legs at the bottom of the bag and fell asleep. We breathed together in silence. I closed my eyes and held my ear against her—one cold ear and one warm. I whispered, "Are you still awake?"

"Mmm-hmm," she sniffled. Her nose was running. I handed her my handkerchief.

"You always have a handkerchief, LC," she said.

"I had bad allergies when I was a kid," I said. "The kids used to do imitations of me blowing my nose. It was hilarious. . . ." I'd let her call me LC because of the sweet rise in her voice on the *C*. It was tenderly wearing down the gruff LC I'd been hearing my whole life.

"At least you weren't held back," she said. "I was already the tallest kid in class, then they held me back a year. I was Gigantor Girl."

"Nah, you're my sweet, sweet, Slim," I said. "And I love you, by the way."

Love. Two years with old whatshername had done little to give me much insight into what that meant. I hadn't wanted to give her up out of embarrassment as much as anything else. Alba was a small school. Everybody knew what was what, but Slim didn't care. She believed in a lot of things, but she did not believe in ghosts. She believed in opening up to the future like a giant sunflower facing the sun.

We finally fell asleep, then woke with dew on our faces, the sleeping bags damp with it. She was red and I was blue, and we were zippered together in Pine River Park, where no camping was allowed. Then we lived happily ever after. . . .

I was back in Warren for Christmas break when one of my hippie house-mates called me with the news. I drove straight back up to school, me and Mudboy in my old Satellite. I took the back roads so I wouldn't have to pass the spot of the accident, though I wasn't sure exactly where that was. Snow blew over the flat, straight back roads of mid-Michigan as if no roads existed at all. I was crying, Mudboy licking my face as if he understood human grief. If only licking each other's faces was enough, but it truly was not.

When I finally get to Alba, first thing I do is find Gina, and we fall into ragged grief together. I just changed tenses, I know, but I'm suddenly there now. Gina's short, maybe five foot four. I'm hugging her and crying down into her hair and staring forward into the space where Kim's face should be. I know that sounds stupid. It was the first time I felt like a piece of the world was missing forever.

Here's where I should offer redemption. To suggest she didn't die in vain, that I became a stronger person, that I dedicated myself to trying to live a life she would've been proud of. But I was an amateur at grief. The coach should have left me on the bench and told me to watch and try and learn a thing or two. Not standing at the free-throw stripe with the game on the line.

Gina and I spent that night together. Yeah, and we had sex too. Fast, wild sex. And then again. But all I felt was one sharp pain. Like a blackboard not being erased, but being blown up into a thousand brittle black pieces. I let Mudboy outside and forgot about him. When I left the next morning, Gina pulled me to her and whispered softly, "Don't ever come back," and I think I understood. She kissed a tear from my cheek and sent me out the door.

When I walked out into the cold on the grayest, cloudiest morning in the history of the world, Alba, Michigan, version, Mudboy was gone, but when I got back to my house, he was waiting on the front stoop, wagging his little butt off. Dumb dog knew his own way home, trusted me to return.

Charles did tell Robin to fuck off, but she wouldn't come to the door, so he had to yell it from the street. Which was okay back in Warren, yelling from the street. Slim got away from the yelling because of the financial generos-ity of a grandmother who painted watercolors in her basement. Slim was going to be a teacher of little kids in her soft candle voice. Her smile would light up a generation or two. Would have lit up. Maybe/would/could have. If she could've passed that one math class. If that community college class would've transferred. If a full moon lit up the river on graduation night. If she'd believed in ghosts. If she had simply lived.

Slim Kim. The mystery of her long strides. Leaves in her hair. Once she slept on the floor with Mudboy instead of on the bed with me because *I was such a smart-ass and when was I ever going to grow up and stop being so cynical?* I never felt so alone as I did that night on the mattress by myself.

Growing up made me *more* cynical, like it does to most people. I keep waiting for the reconciliation of the unfinished. It's like if somebody writes you a note on a tiny piece of paper and rolls it very, very tight. Then she puts a pinhole in an egg and blows all the egg out. Then she puts that tight stick of paper into the pinhole and she says it's a message for you someday when she's gone. And then she's gone and nobody knows what the hell you're talking about when you ask if anyone found an egg in her room, her family wondering, who the hell are you? So you never find out. The idea of the egg lasts forever, this little oval hollow in your heart. You get married, you have your own kids, your hair turns a distinguished gray, and you never become your father's boss, and you never sleep down by the river, any river, ever again, in a red-and-blue double sleeping bag.

When I graduated, I gave Mudboy away—Charles took him, and he spent the rest of his life in a safe, fenced-in yard in Warren, Michigan. I hadn't taken very good care of him—that's probably obvious by now. He'd become a burden, chewing up my books and records, alone in the house I shared while he waited for me to return from chewing up things myself, from being a jerk, assuming there was always time to rewrite the paper, get a better grade. Maybe I should have tried hugging trees first before driving out to Riverdale and taking him from a dry barn and into a rainy afternoon after whatshername dumped me. Mudboy had been an impulsive mistake— one of my consistent weak spots, those impulses. Charles was wrong about thinking. Stopping to think things over was something I did learn. But I was a slow learner. I was a slow dreamer.

I should have been held back.

SCENIC OUTLOOKS

I REMEMBER ONLY ONE VACATION DURING ALL MY YEARS ON PLANET Detroit, though my parents had photographic evidence of me as a baby at Sleeping Bear Sand Dunes looking marooned, disconsolate, in the middle of all that sand. It could've been the surface of the moon, a photo doctored like my father claimed they did at NASA.

My father had great faith in the power of *they*. *They* were always putting the screws to us, raising taxes, gas prices, insurance. In my father's dictionary, *they* had the longest entry, and that entry was blank, for he defined it at his whim. *They were out to get us* was his motto, and I would've had it carved on his tombstone if *they* hadn't already ripped us off for everything else connected to his funeral.

Yeah, I'm a chimp off the old block, as he used to say. I liked chimps, so I didn't mind. Chimps always seem to be imagining they're having a good time—something we weren't very good at—thus, the one family vacation that I remember was a complete disaster.

Michigan's full of lakes, not just the "great" ones. We've got a lot of little inland puddles circled with shacks called cottages and owned and managed by obese men in ball hats with one physical deformity that paid off big for them in a court of law. Or so it seemed, once we arrived at Carl's Kabins on Tea Lake. My father swore that a Guy from Work came here every year and loved it.

My father's antidote to what the *they* of the world were doing to him was to take the sage advice of one of his fellow line workers at the Chrysler plant who was in the same sorry state. Even after he retired, he continued to go to the plant barber, who my father believed should be running the country.

"Why'd he change the *C* on 'Cabin' but not the *C* on 'Carl'?" my brother Randy asked.

"It's all about marketing," my father said, as if he knew something. "Just by getting you to ask that question, he's already got you interested in the place."

Randy was always getting our father riled up with questions from the backseat or dinner table. He often was sent to his room to eat, which was also my room. Randy was a sloppy eater—particularly pissed off and isolated—so our bedroom smelled of moldy spaghetti half the time. The other half smelled like our teenage funk. I'm not sure what was worse. Randy was fifteen, and I was thirteen.

"It's our last chance to go on vacation with the boys," our mother had pleaded until our father gave in. It was really already too late for me and Randy to enjoy a good, wholesome family vacation. We didn't know how.

The Guy from Work had a boat, it turned out, and was primarily interested in fishing. He had no family. He went up with a group of old friends from high school, and they drank beer with Carl and went fishing. They laughed at each other's farts and had a fine time.

Randy and I still laughed at each other's farts, but we could've done that at home, where Randy was in hot pursuit of Gena Martini from over on Dallas Street. As Randy explained it, Gena could be undiscriminating in her displays of affection, and he was worried that a week away might get him erased from the slate of her attention.

Our father had taken the scenic route to Carl's, driving up along the Lake Huron coast. He insisted on pulling into every scenic lookout along the lakeshore and making us get out and look. Then, he'd take various photos of us looking surly into the camera with whatever scenic vista as a backdrop.

The plan was for us to spend a night in a motel—something we'd never done, and our parents hadn't done since their honeymoon in Atlantic City, a long weekend while my father was home on leave from the Army. *They'd* ruined his life by sending him to Vietnam, where his feet nearly rotted off and he saw people die.

"The draft was fucked up, but if they bring it back, you boys are going," he told us.

"Yeah, to Canada," Randy said, then took his spaghetti into our room.

It turned out that it was the weekend of the Port Huron to Mackinac boat race, and all the motels along the lake had their NO VACANCY signs lit up in the growing dark. We ended up sleeping in the car in a rest stop until an enormous state trooper knocked on our window with his enormous flashlight and told us to move on.

"They had to plan their damn race on the same day. . . ." Our father didn't even finish. Randy glowered in the backseat.

"We're having some fun now," he said and looked at me.

"Oh yeah," I said. "Some fun."

Carl greeted my father like an old friend, which was understandable, considering most of his cottages sat vacant. It turned out Carl greeted everyone as an old friend, particularly those who came to buy drugs. I guess he supplemented his income to get him through the off-season, though it looked like every season was the off-season at Carl's.

"A friend of Mitch's is a friend of mine," Carl said. "Though don't be setting any cabins on fire like your old friend, Mitch." He might have been one-quarter joking, not even half joking, because Randy and I saw char marks on Cabin 6.

We never met Mitch, or any of the other Guys from Work. We knew some nights when our father came home late and beery that he'd been "out with the boys," though the boys were never invited over—our house was so tiny, Randy and I never had our own friends over either. We hung out on the street, even in winter, which is maybe why we were already drinkers ourselves the year we went off to Carl's Kabins.

Our cabin was even smaller than that house, and it smelled like dead fish, since it sat next to the fish-cleaning stand, which seemed to be a very popular rental for local raccoons who spooked Randy and me, standing on their back legs and hissing at us like vicious carnival toys in some horror movie we may have seen previews for.

Randy and I shared a room at home, but at Carl's we had to share a bed. We slept far apart on opposite edges, our bodies as stiff as those crib rails you slide up to keep the little rascals in, as we tried to hold on against the deep sag in the middle that pulled us together.

Our mother cooked pancakes the first morning, though Carl didn't have much cooking gear. She used a fireplace shovel to flip them with, so they tasted a little ashy, but since our father smoked we were used to ashes.

"They get you hooked, then they kill you," he used to say about cigarettes and cigarette makers and all involved parties. Our mother was always after him to quit, and he did, right before he died. His prophecies were often true, though he made few of them.

"Good pahncakes, Ma," Randy said. "They shtick to the woof a my mouf."

I was busy guzzling a glass of milk so I wouldn't choke—the tiny local grocery did not have syrup.

"What do they put on their pancakes up here so they don't need syrup?" my father asked. He'd been trying to put a good face on the Guy from Work Mitch's hot tip on an inexpensive resort vacation.

That night, Randy and I came back drunk after hitchhiking into the tiny town of Mars, Michigan, where we had cadged the proverbial old guy in a baseball hat to buy for us.

"They got 'em here too, ain't that somethin,'" I said.

"They're everywhere, you dope," Randy said, pulling that older brother shit on me like he was the veteran of the world, though I'd actually had a real girlfriend the previous summer, Brenda Macklin, who had blossomed two doors down from us while Randy was off with his one sad *Hustler* magazine and his lunkhead friends whose idea of a joke was punching each other in the shoulder. My father liked Randy's friends and would show them knife tricks and ways to win at poker on the rare occasion that he was home.

Randy and all his friends ended up in the factory too. I myself spent time there, but, being two years younger, got laid off when Chrysler hit that wall they seem to hit every ten or fifteen years. Like some stubborn dolt, they keep ramming their gas-guzzling truck into that wall, expecting it to collapse, but it never does. Eventually, they seem to find a way to drive around it, but by then they're once again behind the Japanese or the Germans or whoever.

I've never been a ball-hat-wearing drunk buying for the kiddies in the parking lot, by the way. I moved away to the tropical paradise of Wheeling, West Virginia, home of the Mud Sandwich and other delicacies to be had at Red's Roadside Paradise, if you're ever in the vicinity. Randy has all the family photos now, since our mother is blind, so this is all from my warped memory.

Anyway, we came back drunk, stumbling in, laughing, our parents sitting around the campfire with Carl, whose name was once indeed Karl. People told him it sounded too German, he said. Randy got in an animated discussion with Carl about this, until apparently it became obvious that his animation was not Karl-induced, and our father yanked us both back to our cabin and gave us one of his famous talking-tos, while back at the campfire, Carl asked our mother if she'd like to shimmy in his shanty after the old man nodded off. She declined.

After he died, our mother told us just about everything we never wanted to know. To this day, she'll call up just to say, "Did I tell you I smoked marijuana once?"

Randy and I don't talk much on the phone. Our wives talk to each other, and they give us synopses with footnotes. For example:

"Hey, Bro."

"Yo, Randy."

"Happy Birthday, dude."

"Thanks, man."

"Whacha doin' with it?"

"Cake and shit. . . . Hey, it looks like Wendy wants to get on the line."

"I'll get Mary Beth. Have a good one."

Since he almost died in a motorcycle accident two years ago, Randy's started telling me he loves me before signing off, and I tell him back because the old man never told us before he died. Though he did take us on that vacation to Carl's Kabins, we remind each other.

The next day, which turned out to be the only sunny day that week, Randy and I figured on swimming some. Carl had no beach. We jumped off the dock into algae and quicksand. Randy and I stared at each other while we sank into the muck and weeds, then we turned around and looked at the rest of the lake, hoping there might be a girl in a bikini somewhere in that sad cup of tea.

We had to rinse the muck off our legs with a hose. I don't know where Carl found that picture that was on the brochure. Probably over on Lake Huron, where they did have sandy beaches, beaches you could look down on from scenic overlooks, or *outlooks,* as my father called them, snapping yet another photo.

That afternoon we drove to town in search of ice cream. My father stopped at a pay phone outside a convenience store to call Mitch and find out where the fun was.

"Ask him where the babes are!" Randy shouted into the old graffitied phone booth, but he still got to eat with us that night. "They all look like lesbians in that store," Randy grumbled.

"You wouldn't know a lesbian if one bit you on the ass," I said.

"Why would a lesbian bite me on the ass, you dope," he said.

Nobody came out in our high school. We didn't even know what it meant—coming out from where to where? Randy was so convinced of his charms that he believed anyone who did not succumb must be a lesbian. His friend Gorpy turned out to be gay, but he didn't emerge until his thirties, and that was after he'd been married twice. Randy avoided Gorpy after that.

Carl had a meth lab going on the premises, the state police would later determine. That explained the ammonia smell that blew on the breeze from

Carl's own Kabin up near the road—it sure wasn't from Carl cleaning the place. We didn't see him much during the day. His German shepherd almost ripped my father's head off when he surprised Carl Thursday morning, wanting to ask him for advice on good fishing spots.

We knew we were in trouble when the old man started fishing. He'd never fished in his life. We knew he'd be wanting company, so Randy and I took off in one of Carl's battered rowboats, heading straight across the lake, assuming there was a good side to the lake that was the opposite of where we were located. A land of sandy beaches and bikinis and beer and somebody playing the guitar and bongos. Girls doing the limbo.

We heard our father shouting at us, but we were far enough away so we could pretend not to hear. The lake appeared to be lined with other versions of Carl's Kabins:

Kevin's Cottages. Bunk's Beach Houses, Harry's Hide-a-Way, Fartin' and Fishin'. Well, I made that last one up.

We did see a pretty girl lying on a dock, but she gave us the finger just for saying, "Hey."

She was smiling though. "Maybe it's a regional thing," I whispered, rowing closer.

"Hey, is that a regional sign of affection?" Randy shouted.

"It's a sign known the world over," she said. "No affection in it."

"What do you do for fun around here," I asked, trying my own charming smile.

"You're doing it, big boy," she said. "Row around till you get tired, then if you're lucky, you sink."

"Ha," I said.

"Ha ha," Randy said.

She was older than she first looked, older than us—maybe even married. I steered back toward the open water.

Randy eventually took a crack at rowing himself, he was that bored. "Let a man take over," he said. We shifted positions. I leaned over the front of the boat and looked into the water for fish.

"I hope dad catches something," I said.

"Why?" Randy asked.

I was suddenly sad. The long, slow days at Lake Limbo had pulled me down. It was the most time I'd spent with my father in my entire life. The most I would ever spend. An entire week. And he was fishing. And he was catching nothing. Certainly not us.

"Something to cheer him up, man," I said.

"He's always like this," Randy said, pulling hard on the oars.

"Is he?" I asked.

"I think so," he said.

"I don't know if he knows who to blame this one on," I said. "He seems confused."

"*They*," Randy said. "*They* did it."

The way he said *they*—a dead-on impression of the old man now that Randy's voice had changed—made me laugh despite the sadness.

When we got close to shore, I shouted, "Any bites, Dad?"

He startled, nearly knocking his cardboard tub of worms off the dock.

"They're hiding on me," he said. When he reeled in his line, there was no worm on it.

"They stole my bait," he said, though as much as he knew about fishing, the worm could've just swum right off the hook. "Mitch says you gotta use a boat to get the big ones. Didn't you boys hear me hollering at you?"

"We just thought you were excited to see us go," Randy said, but he couldn't get another rise out of our father that week. It was like, given enough time, our father would have lost his edge completely, opened up to us, even though we had our own edges now. Randy was like a bully, disappointed the kid he was picking on wouldn't fight back. He either said "You're hopeless" or "It's hopeless" as he pulled up the oars and I jumped on the dock. He walked away without me.

"Not biting, eh Mitch?" Carl said.

"I am not Mitch. My friend is Mitch."

"Right, right," Carl said. My father waited for Carl to remember his name—Bob—but Carl did not care enough to find it.

My father could fix anything in the world that could be fixed with tools, but he could not catch a fish.

I could tell my father was humiliated that week. His shoulders slumped as he sat in one of Carl's splintery deck chairs in his antique bathing suit. The elastic had dried out, and the suit was constantly sagging to reveal his butt crack. It was too much pressure on one week of his life. We, his sons, had already left him behind while he'd been busy working overtime and fixing things. I felt his humiliation myself on the silent, stinky shore of that brown lake. Not enough to sit on the dock with him in the heat of the day—even I knew that wasn't a good time to fish—and pretend to have some deep father-and-son moments. I'd be as bad as Randy in a couple of years, lashing out at him, crumbing up our room.

"Be cool, stay in school," he always told us, as if that was something he'd made up himself. He had not stayed in school. He had gotten my mother pregnant with Randy and married her and dropped out to work in the factory until he was drafted. I was born while he was in Vietnam. Right after he got back, we took that trip to the sand dunes. In the photos, my father is slim and muscled. He looks both defeated and able to take on the world. The defeat part was in his eyes. Though he loved taking photos himself, he always hated having his own photo taken. He might've become gun-shy after the war. He kept his old Army stuff in a wooden box, and in that box was a picture of his platoon, and in tiny, delicate script, he wrote "dead" beneath half the men.

Randy and I got in the only serious fight of our lives that week. I've been dancing around the ring of that fight like a dubious contender, like the guy who knows he's getting knocked out but can't decide whether he should just plunge in and take the fall or try to survive another round or two.

I'd walked in on him masturbating. Those doors at Carl's didn't entirely close—everything was out of whack. Randy jumped off the toilet and yanked up his pants.

"Fucking pervert. What are you doing, spying on me? You all excited now?"

I should've just walked out, but I laughed and said something untrue, suggesting that I was way ahead of him and that Brenda was still servicing me whenever I so desired, and that he was a loser jack-off who'd be jacking off his whole life because no girl would ever want to come near him, and not even that whore Gena Martini was going to give him anything, even though she'd stooped so low as to take on Gorpy.

Something like that. Perhaps I didn't get a chance to finish that thought as he punched me in the nose and we wrestled, bouncing off the walls like we were in some WWF cage match. We cracked a piece of Carl's cheap plywood, tumbling into the tiny main room, then out the screen door, where we really began to wail on each other. Our parents weren't there to break it up. They may have been minigolfing, a step below fishing in pitifulness. Carl wandered over to stand and watch, and we got embarrassed. I hated the guy and did not want to offer him some kind of perverse free entertainment. Randy was getting the best of me anyway, so I just backed away and mumbled, "I quit." Randy said nothing. We both knew we'd be in some trouble for the damage, but we weren't going to tell Carl about it. "Fuck you, Carl," I wanted to say, but I just glared at his smug face, then smacked the screen door closed behind me.

You might think a guy like Carl was one of us and not a *they*. I believe he counted on people giving him the benefit of the doubt on that. Unlike my father, I was beginning to understand that *they* had spies among us. The job of these spies was to fuck us up so we'd be wailing on each other while *they* counted their money. Guys like Carl got their traitor's cut and were happy. This is a rough translation of what I learned in college for the benefit of Randy, who still doesn't get it, though I love him dearly, and we never talked about that fight. I blame it on boredom and disappointment and shame. The house in Detroit was the best we could do, the best we could ever do, so my father was right in staying home, using his vacation time to paint it, fix it, build a bathroom in the basement for us, make his own home a place that would never embarrass him.

We were leaving Saturday morning. On Friday night, my father gave us each ten dollars and told us to have a good time and be careful. We guessed he was allowing us to get drunk, though he wouldn't be putting on the baseball hat himself. He'd be staying at the cottage with my mother and getting good and hammered by his own lonesome while my mother adjusted the rabbit ears on the old TV, hoping to bring in something besides some fuzzy

PBS affiliate from outer space. Something with commercials, something that she could dream about without shame.

A Friday night, but hardly any cars on the road, and nobody stopped to give us a ride. We walked into town, accumulating mosquito bites as we went. Main Street was the tiny grocery, a closed movie theater, a diner (also closed), a hardware store, a liquor store, and a few other storefronts of indistinguishable purpose. We stood outside the liquor store for an hour before a county cop chased us away.

"Candy store's down the street," he shouted at us behind the bright glare of his spotlight, but there was no candy store in that town.

When Randy and I weigh in on our one vacation, even now we can't admit how bad it was. *The bugs were bad,* he'll say. Or, *the weather was bad,* I'll say. *Forces beyond our control.* Or *Mom flipped pancakes with a fireplace shovel*— it's okay to say that, and we laugh, and our wives and kids laugh a little, because they know their grandmother, in her seventies now.

On the way home, my father found yet another scenic route to take, conjuring roads from his crisp new map. He seemed quietly determined to get some good photos, some evidence to take in to work so he wouldn't seem like a sap for getting taken in by Mitch's bullshit. We did not complain. In fact, Randy and I even began looking for the signs for scenic overlooks and called them out to my father in the front seat. We'd hop out of the car and pose on either side of our mother, big smiles on our faces. It was like we were all doing a job together, fixing something that was broken.

SHOCKS AND STRUTS

IT STARTED OUT LIKE ONE OF THOSE JANGLY SPRINGSTEEN ANTHEMS with the heavy drums and organ kicking in, but it ended up repeating the same words over and over again. You couldn't even understand them, though the singer was so passionate and possessed he looked like he was trying to vomit up tiny animals.

"Heavy shit," Bobby said.

"Let me spit?" Jill asked. "Yeah, maybe that's it."

The bar was called Shocks and Struts, on Six Mile near Mound Road, just two miles from the Chrysler stamping plant Bobby worked at, but he'd never been inside the place before. The band was called Rocket Socket. He didn't know what that meant, but he knew he'd never see these young rockers again.

"Wanna dance?" Jill looked at him skeptically.

"I don't want to throw my back out. I'd never hear the end of it from the guys at work—disability on the dance floor."

"'Disability on the Dance Floor.' It could be a new dance craze or something. Like the 'Tighten Up.'"

"Archie Bell and the Drells." He smiled at Jill. She knew he loved to dredge up rock 'n' roll trivia. He was proud to have some knowledge that set him apart from all the other shop rats.

The song ended with one of those rock 'n' roll *oomphs,* dragged out so the drummer's messing with your head a bit, making you think it's the last note when he's got a few more to shoot out. Kind of like a good orgasm, Bobby thought.

"Maybe we should leave," he said quickly, before the next song could get started. But then he noticed that the singer was wiping his face with a T-shirt a young woman had just removed. Bobby strained to see some flesh from where they stood near the back of the bar. The band had a following, that much was clear. Teenage girls with fake IDs and guys who were only there for the girls. A scene all too familiar from Bobby's younger days, getting shit-faced at the bar, staring at the dance floor, waiting for the miracle of some girl in tight jeans giving him the time of day. Bobby had been pushing fifty, but now fifty was pushing him. The next song was starting up.

"Bring her up on stage," Bobby shouted.

"What?" Jill asked.

"'Turn the Page,'" he quickly shouted. "Remember that old Bob Seger song?"

"I always wanted it to be S-e-e-g-e-r. With another *e,* he would've been unstoppable." Jill was three years younger than Bobby, the same age as his brother Steve.

"That's just the Detroit in you talking. He needed one of Springsteen's *e*'s. These guys need *both* them *e*'s. . . . Let's get out of here."

"What about the lovebirds? We can't just leave them here." Steve and his new girlfriend, whose name Bobby had already forgotten, were in the middle of the crowded chaos of the dance floor. It looked dangerous out there.

"They deserve each other. They deserve this shitty music. Look at her— she looks ready to take her shirt off too. My brother ought to be ashamed of himself going for jailbait like that."

"She's old enough to get in," Jill said.

"Well, he's old enough to know better," Bobby replied. "Me, I'm just here to look."

She smacked him hard in the shoulder, and he winced and grinned. Jill was solid. She could take care of herself and, for a time, had taken care of Bobby too. He put on his old black leather jacket, pulled out of the back of the closet for the occasion, careful to slip his arms in without doing more damage to the already-torn lining. "I'll tell him we're leaving," he said.

"I'll come too," Jill said, but he waved her away as the crowd closed behind him.

Muscling and weaving through the wriggling bodies, Bobby found his way to Steve. In the rock 'n' roll bars of Detroit, dancing hadn't evolved in thirty years: swivel and shake, stomp and swing. Steve's girlfriend had certain assets, no question about it. Her long blonde hair twirled as she danced with clenched fists and grinned maniacally at Steve. Bobby paused to take it in before grabbing his brother's shoulder. They were stoned on something, but Bobby wasn't sure what.

"We're splitting now, Bro. Good luck."

Steve turned to him. "You can't go yet. You've barely had time to talk to Mindy." Mindy, that was her name.

"We're too old for this shit," Bobby shouted in his ear. "You can tell Mindy it's past my bedtime."

"Hey, man," Steve said.

"Look, we're leaving. That's the short version. If you want the long version, you're gonna have to come visit us some day when you're straight."

Steve rolled his eyes and turned back to Mindy. Bobby walked away without looking back.

Steve had been divorced six months. One of the causes for the divorce had been his screwing around, so it seemed like the marriage had already been over much, much longer. Bobby had covered for him on many occasions. Steve's ex wife, Sara-no-h, blamed Bobby for pretty much everything. After all, he'd gotten divorced first, and he was the older brother, she reasoned—as if brothers still copycatted each other in middle age. Bobby was already remarried to Jill. And Bobby had gotten straight. And Steve had not.

"Are you jealous?" Jill asked when they finally shouldered open the dented metal door and stepped out of the bar and into the cool quiet air. The gravel beneath their feet sounded like little microphones. Bobby frowned. His ears were ringing, and he wanted to hear every little thing for the rest of his life. Losing hearing to a band that bad was like some form of ear suicide.

"Jealous? C'mon, Jill. Little Miss Fluffy—okay, she's cute in a porno kind of way, but twenty years difference—that's insane. Steve's hair dye is gonna rub off on the sheets, and then it'll be all over."

"Little Miss Fluffy? I thought her name was Candi Muffin?"

Bobby laughed. "Candi Muffin. . . . Wasn't she a stripper down at the National Burlesque when we were kids?"

"I wouldn't know, big boy. I was spending a lot of my time in the convent back then."

Though Jill had not literally spent time in a convent, her parents had tried to keep her away from boys like Bobby. When her first marriage ended, she rejoined the Catholic church, simply ignoring the excommunication rule, and started taking the sacraments again. She and Bobby couldn't get married in church, but he wouldn't have gone for that anyway. They got married at the JOP. Steve was supposed to be one of the witnesses, but he didn't show. Steve showed up when he wanted something, not when anyone else was counting on him. He and Bobby had no other living family beyond some distant aunts and uncles who had disappeared after their parents died.

Jill said the church gave her comfort, allowed her to move forward. She let Bobby kid her about religion, but every Sunday she went to mass by herself. Like she would tomorrow morning, Bobby imagined, while he slept in and read the paper and drank a pot of coffee and soaked in the peace and quiet as if he were making up for a lifetime deficit.

"Busty Russell, now *she* was a stripper. Sixty-two-inch chest, and that was in the days before silicone."

"You go out to the bar and turn sixteen again. I can't take you anywhere."

"If I'm sixteen, what does that make Steve?"

"We're stuck with Steve. Family means being stuck with—"

"With assholes," Bobby sighed. He was getting flashbacks to that old drunken loneliness that had taken him home so many nights for so many years. Stepping out of the bar at closing time, defeated and alone. A six-pack-to-go under one arm to finish off the night back home.

"Sorry, hon," he said. He put his arm around her, gave her a tight squeeze. "Felt a little something tugging at me back there."

"I'll give you a tug," she said.

"I think Steve's doing coke again."

"You *think?* Come on—it's not rocket science."

"Staying clean, now *that's* fucking rocket science."

As they crossed the street to their car, two jumpy young hoods intercepted them between parked cars. The first guy—a young punk a foot taller than Bobby—body-slammed him onto a red Firebird, one of those fancy jobs with the flaming bird on the hood.

But Bobby couldn't fly away, so it looked like he was going to get his ass kicked. He'd been in his share of street fights, bar fights, long ago. He'd sworn them off, though he still carried an edge with him, a wariness that quickly took offense. It ran in the family. It came in handy at work.

"Hey!" Jill shouted, reaching up to pull on the punk's shoulders, but the other guy yanked her off.

The punk paused, pinning Bobby down as he struggled to get a hand free, some leverage for fighting back.

"This is the dude, right?" he asked the guy holding Jill.

"Yeah, sure. Steve Cogan, right?"

"No!" Jill shouted.

"Yeah. Yeah, that's me," Bobby said quickly. "Just curious—what did I do to deserve this?"

"*This?* We ain't done nothing yet," the one on top of him said, laughing a forced tough-guy laugh that made Bobby want to puke. The guy turned to his partner. "Who's the old broad?"

"Hell if I know. But this is the guy—he came out of the bar, it looks like him, and he says it's him."

"It's his brother, you assholes," Jill shouted. Bobby gave her a look.

Then the other guy—one of those short, chippy guys Bobby had hated all his life—stepped forward and punched Bobby in the nose. His head crashed back against the hood again. Bobby grunted. He felt blood spurt down into his mouth. Maybe it was oozing out of the back of his head too, but he couldn't feel back there.

Jill screamed. The other guy put his hand over her mouth. She elbowed him in the gut, shook herself free, and ran. Bobby kneeled the guy on top of him in the balls and twisted off the hood. They were about fifty yards off Mound, a busy six-laner that ran out into the distant suburbs past a long series of auto plants and tool-and-die shops. Bobby was trying to follow her, though he'd never been fast, and he was still staggered from the punch. Jill slowed for Bobby to catch up.

"Faster!" he shouted. "Get to Mound—make a fucking scene!"

The two thugs chased him. The old Bobby wanted to turn and fight. He felt the rush his own blood gave him, but he was old Bobby, not *the* old Bobby. Plus, who knew what Steve had done this time.

A week ago Sunday, Bobby had called Steve. He hadn't heard from him in a couple of months. Sometimes that was a good sign, but he figured he'd better check in.

"I got a girlfriend," Steve said. "It's serious."

Bobby scoffed. "How long you been seeing her?"

"Long enough. She's fucking beautiful. All my fantasies come true."

"Right," Bobby said. "Does she come with a winning lottery ticket? That's a dangerous thing, fantasies coming true. You ever see anybody rub a genie and come out of it okay on the other end?"

Steve had been out of work for eight months, a casualty of the last round of layoffs at Ford's. His unemployment had run out. He had too much time on his hands and not enough money. A bad combination for anyone, but particularly Steve, whose laundry list of vices had prompted Jill to refer to him as Steve Anonymous, as if he was addiction personified. "Okay, why don't you bring her over to dinner this weekend?"

"She's not a dinner-date kind of girl."

"Bowling?"

"Dancing. Music. She likes to party."

Bobby paused. "Shit, Steve. You want us to come out and 'party' with you and this girl? We do our partying in front of the TV these days. Going to a bar is like going to the dentist. A dentist who has the best fucking drugs to ease the pain, but we know we can't have any."

Bobby stumbled to the cement, and the punks caught up with him.

"Hit me again, mother fucker," Bobby roared, standing up to face them. Miraculously, they backed off. Maybe he was close enough to Mound to be seen, standing in the middle of the street, or maybe the madman facing them seemed too crazy, or maybe they'd made their point, enough of a point to get whatever their payment was. Or maybe they heard the siren approaching. Jill had stopped traffic on Mound on a Saturday night—not an easy feat. The neon lights of the Bel-Air Motel across the street flashed on and off in their cheap fifties kind of way. Bobby's thick shoulders curled in on each other in pain. It was cold, and he had no business being out at 1 A.M. He closed his eyes and silently cursed his brother.

The cops had a roll of paper towels in the trunk of the squad car, and one of them handed it to Bobby. He tilted his head back and wiped off or sucked in as much blood as he could. While Jill looked on warily, he told the police what happened without mentioning Steve: these two guys had simply jumped them. In that neighborhood, the police didn't question it. Bobby was stone-cold sober and looked too old to get into a bar fight. Nobody'd gotten shot, so it was a minor skirmish they were quickly bored by. They didn't even offer to take him to the hospital. They wrote up a quick report, said they'd cruise the neighborhood, and took off.

Jill drove him to the ER at Henry Ford, and they waited in the long Saturday-night lineup of drug overdoses, shootings, accident victims, and hysterical family members. They sat, subdued and furious.

"Jesus Christ, what'd he do this time?" Jill muttered over and over. "Why did *you* do this? He needs to take his own beatings. . . ."

Bobby grimaced, his long legs twitching beneath the orange, cracked, plastic waiting-room chair. Steve had been in trouble before. Petty stuff—small drug deals, fencing stolen electronic equipment, etc. Since losing his job, he'd been elusive and distracted. The only criminal activity Bobby was interested in was what he saw on TV every night, the neatly constructed dramas with their perfectly timed resolutions. Taking a punch in his little brother's name, then editing that name from the police report—why *had* he done it? Steve needed help, was spiraling down below ground zero, and taking a hit for him seemed like the only concrete thing Bobby could do to help—something Steve didn't have a say in, couldn't object to.

"Stupid," he said aloud, thinking of both Steve and himself. It was time for one of those brother-to-brother talks. The thought of that intensified the pain in his face, and in his ribs each time he breathed: Steve, Steve. Pain, pain. And, by the way, where did he meet Miss Fluffy? He closed his eyes. Voices from the confrontational talk show on the TV mounted above him mixed with the voices of the stoned, the pained, and the grieving. He asked if he could change the channel, but no one answered. No one had the remote.

It was just one punch, but it could've been more. His nose had not been broken—Bobby had a nose of steel. But he had a large bruise under one cheek, a fat lip, and probably a cracked rib or two. Exhausted, he tried to steady his shaking hands as a nurse finally cleaned his wounds.

"Past my bedtime," he mumbled as they got back in the car. What *had* Steve done, Bobby wondered. Owed money? Stole drugs? Pissed off his ex wife? Maybe Miss Fluffy was Mrs. Fluffy and had a Mister who was not so fluffy?

When they were young, Bobby let Steve borrow his ID to buy booze and hit the bars. The partying Cogan boys'd had a wild run for a lot of years, running right through their first marriages. They still looked like brothers, but Bobby's hair was gray. Steve insisted on dyeing his with some cheap stuff from the drugstore. It looked like the color of a weird brown crayon, but in the darkness of a bar, it looked just good enough for the likes of Miss Fluffy. Tomorrow—wait, today was tomorrow, he realized—*later today,* he'd call Steve and ask him *what the fuck.* There was a little bit of truth in just about everything, and what hurt Bobby the most was that part of him *was* still Steve Cogan.

When Bobby woke up, he had no idea what time it was. He could usually tell by the traffic. They lived on the Detroit side of Eight Mile Road, close enough to hear the whoosh of the eight lanes of traffic and judge the time of day by the volume of the whoosh. In the summer, with the windows open, they could smell exhaust fumes. But on Sunday, the traffic was muted all day long.

He'd fallen asleep with a bag of ice on his face, and it had melted over his pillow and onto the sheets. He shook with a chill. Early October, and they'd been debating whether to turn the furnace on yet. He was going to turn it on today.

He looked at the bedside alarm clock: noon. Jill was up and dressed, getting ready for the last mass of the day at one o'clock. She'd already called Steve, but he either was asleep or not answering. Bobby didn't have a mobile phone. These days, he was usually at work or at home. Not mobile. Jill had one. She worked as a sales rep for an auto parts supplier and was often on the road. Steve had one and used it as his only phone, to conduct whatever business he was conducting these days, wherever he was.

"Let me try," Bobby said, hungover with pain. It'd take him at least a week to feel normal, and there was no telling when he'd *look* normal again. He flinched at the hallway mirror as he passed. The smell of coffee, which usually brought stability to his mornings, made him nauseous.

"What, you think you've got magic powers to make him pick up?"

"Remind me never to get hit in the face again. I forgot how much it hurts."

Jill gave him a big hug, and he flinched. "Ribs."

"Sorry, Bobby. I was scared last night. Real scared."

"I'm still scared," Bobby said. "I never used to be scared."

"Being scared means being smart some times."

"Well, I've never been that kind of scared."

Just then the phone rang. Not the house phone, but Jill's cell. They looked at each other. She scrambled to get it, and her purse spilled, makeup and change and keys flying across the linoleum floor. Bobby winced.

"You'll be late for church," he said as she picked up the phone.

"Yes," he heard her say. "Yes, that's me. . . . That can't be," she said. "That can't be. He's right here with me," she said.

Someone was in Harper Hospital under Bobby's name. Bobby thought maybe Steve still had a piece of his old ID, or had stolen something more recent, anticipating the need to fuck over his older brother. Maybe the thugs, Big Bill and Little Bill, had gone in the bar to have a drink, ran into Steve, and got their minds blown in a way that resulted in some unpleasantness.

"Did they give his condition?" Bobby asked.

"Oh, my *husband's* stable, you'll be happy to know," Jill said. She bit off each word like raw meat.

"I hope he's not using my health insurance," Bobby said. He sighed, and his ribs jolted him again. "You go to church, and I'll deal with the boy. You got time to tape up these ribs for me?"

Jill shook her head and hurried out the door. It looked like she was crying. Jill, wife number two, who got his jokes, who had a bad-girl past to rival his bad-boy past. Their rockets had crash-landed together at an AA meeting, and they'd rekindled the spark they'd briefly created back in high school before stomping it out together. He trusted her with survivor's trust.

"How can I rise from the dead if you're not even gonna wrap me up?" He shouted after her. "Fuck my little brother, but say a prayer for me."

He couldn't lose Jill because of his stupid brother. He couldn't let *her* mix them up. He was the new, improved model, and he wasn't going to let his brother pull him back into some demolition derby where nobody came out undamaged.

Steve had a concussion, so they'd kept him overnight.

Bobby walked into the hospital room. Steve was sitting up, waiting to be released. They'd done all the tests and given him the okay. He looked alright. A cut above one eye, another on his chin. Not much swelling.

Steve looked up. "Oh—shit, Bobby, what the fuck?"

"I thought *you* were Bobby. Doesn't look like it helped you any. I was Steve, and look what it got me. How come Fluffy isn't here looking after you?"

"Mindy . . . Ouch."

"Ouch?"

"Uh . . . This is about her."

"The thugs?"

". . . Her brothers."

"They find you in the bar?"

Steve sighed and closed his eyes. "Listen, I've got a headache, Bro."

Bobby wanted to kick his brother's ass, but his ribs hurt too much. He needed to know what this game was so he wouldn't get hurt again.

"Look at me, asshole. I took a bullet for you last night. Do you understand?" Bobby wanted to scream at his brother like that bad singer in the bar.

"Yeah, but then they got me with another bullet anyway."

"Whose fucking fault is that? What do they have against you and Muffy? Why'd they kick my ass when I was with Jill, then? This whole thing is—what was I thinking, saying I was you?"

"It's the Martian complex, Bro. You can't help being a Martian and sacrificing yourself. You're my fucking hero, did I tell you that?" Steve said sarcastically. He was coming down hard and needed a fix of something.

"Just tell me what's going on before I walk out of here. Unlike you, speaking of bullets, I do not own a gun. The message the boys were meant to deliver was never articulated."

"You're not going to be amused."

"Do I look amused now?"

Steve said he'd been handling some product to get him through this rough patch. Mindy liked the product. Her brothers found Mindy using the product. The brothers did not want their sister to use the product. Sleeping with Steve looked like a sex for drugs deal, some old guy taking advantage of their innocent little sister.

"So who did they think Jill was, some hooker doing tricks for me?" Every time Bobby raised his voice his chest throbbed with pain. "What, she was your girlfriend as long as you kept her fired up?"

"Jill must be hating on me big time."

"Jill's the least of your worries."

"You didn't have to say you were me. Just show them your fucking driver's license."

"I'll do that next time." He paused to try and take a deep breath. "I assure you."

"I didn't even know she had brothers."

Bobby closed his eyes and took short, rapid breaths. "Okay, how much you owe those guys? I don't buy this 'brothers' bullshit. Muffy's just an innocent bystander, am I right? She saw you getting beat up and took off."

"I told you I have a fucking headache."

"It doesn't sound like you should be in any hurry to get out of here—probably the safest place for you right now. Look, this ain't no TV show. The brothers Cogan aren't going out to seek revenge and triumph over the bad guys after the next commercial break."

"I ain't even told you nothing yet," Steve said, falling into a deep sulk.

"Lying to your brother, the one guy who's on your side. Why do you think I stopped doing all this shit?"

"It's not like you're Mr. Clean, Bro."

"There's a thing called the statute of limitations."

"Oh, I could tell Jill some things. . . ."

"You go right ahead," Bobby said.

"Maybe it'd be worth something to you if I didn't."

"What, you trying to blackmail me? Steve, I'm going to leave right now. Don't call. Don't come over. Don't. . . . Don't. . . . You bottom out, give me a call. If you're still alive."

"That's funny," Steve said, stopping Bobby at the door. "It worked with Jill."

Bobby turned sharply and almost passed out from the pain.

"Oh yeah, she's been good for some timely loans." Steve seemed to be reviving, feeding off his own spite.

"I'll kill you myself," Bobby said through gritted teeth, but instead walked off down the antiseptic hallway, stepping around a man with a mop who looked at his face and shook his head. Bobby wondered if the guy was some kind of omen who knew something he didn't. Something coming his way, and maybe it wasn't good.

On the drive home, Bobby decided to confront Jill, if only to convince her that nothing could be so bad that she couldn't tell him.

"You look horrible," she said when he walked in. "Sit down, big guy." She only wore a dress to go to church, and in that dress she looked like someone who would never stoop to marrying someone like Bobby.

He collapsed on their stained leather couch and closed his eyes.

He expected Jill to at least ask how Steve was, but she didn't.

"You looked like a Firebird, spread out on that hood last night. Like a superhero with wings. . . ."

Bobby opened his eyes and stared at her.

"For a second or so, anyway."

"How long were you planning on giving him money?" he asked. He took three breaths, four. Jill turned away and twisted the blinds closed behind him.

"You—you can't believe . . ." she started.

"Then why pay him?"

Jill began to cry softly. "I'm sorry," she said. "I know that's not enough, but I'm sorry."

She was talking like Steve had already told him her secrets. Bobby wasn't sure why he hadn't. But he was sure he didn't want to know them.

"Just promise you'll never give him another dime," Bobby said. He motioned for her to join him on the couch. He'd never been good at forgiveness. At last, she came and sat beside him, carefully leaning against his shoulder.

"I always thought 'Turn the Page' was a bullshit song," he said.

"They're all bullshit songs. That's why you can't listen to the lyrics. You just have to let them wash over you."

"I think . . ." he began. He was thinking of Steve, of the boy in him, of the goodness buried in him. But he needed to let Steve go. When the hospital called, he'd imagined Steve might be dead, and for a second he'd felt a sense of relief. He tried to remember the name of the guy with the wax wings who flew too close to the sun. Is that how Satan lost the battle?

"What does God mean by mercy?" he asked. "How much mercy does each of us have?"

"Mistaken identity," she said. "It can kill you." She pulled away from him slightly. He could feel the absence of warmth against his skin.

"Worse," he said. "It can break your heart."

On the couch, they drifted into each other, and then to sleep, as dusk fell, then darkness. They lay so still that you'd have to strain to hear their breathing. When the phone rang, it rang and rang. In the morning, they were woken by traffic.

THRESHOLD

They sat outside, though it was too cold to sit outside. Icy wind burned their faces. The waitress, holed up inside, chatting with the bartender, studiously ignored them. No one ate outside in Detroit. It was anti-Detroit for a restaurant to even provide outdoor seating unless it involved eating in your car, but the Three Oaks Golf Club had a patio next to the bar-restaurant, and Ricky needed the air. Hazel was back up from Florida, where it was always warm enough to sit outside. She looked like she'd been living outside. Her skin held a dirty ruddiness that Ricky did not remember. It'd only been a year, but she'd aged five. He caught himself staring into the lines around her mouth, where her smile used to be. He knew she would ask for money, just like all the times before. It never worked over the phone—too easy for him to hang up and return to whatever lock he was happily picking, whatever key he was grinding.

"Do I seem doped up?" she asked. Her spilled Coke gleamed like oil on the white plastic table.

Ricky stood up and waved aggressively at the waitress through the tinted windows.

"Why don't you just walk inside and get her?" Hazel asked.

He sat back down. "Compared to what, do you seem doped up?"

"Find some napkins. This shit's going to run off the table." But the Coke remained in its meandering shape, a stagnant river without its source.

"It's going to freeze in a minute, and we can have Coke-sicles. Let's get the hell out of here." Ricky blew on his hands.

"They never got cola popsicles right. They always left this taste in your mouth like bad medicine. Remember?"

"What kind of 'medicine' do you seem to be doped up on?"

She turned away from his gaze. "I like it out here. Good old goose bumps."

"If we just start leaving, she'll come running with the check, just wait and see." Ricky guzzled the rest of his beer. It was early in the year for her to be showing up—April, with Michigan still flashing back to winter, reluctant to let it go.

Brother and sister, Ricky and Hazel. Thirty-seven and thirty-four. Ricky's wife, Shara, would not let Hazel in their house. Ever since five years ago, when her gold necklace disappeared.

Ricky lit up a cigarette, gave one to Hazel and lit it for her, then the two of them slowly walked off the patio and into the parking lot.

"Put it out before we get in the car. Shara thinks I quit."

"Why do you stay with that bitch?" Hazel asked.

"You ask me that every time."

"It's part of the ritual."

"Yeah, then you ask for money."

"Nah, I have to tell you a story first."

"I don't know if I want to hear your story this time." He was trying to think of a way to bring up her haggard appearance.

"Five years is a long time to be pissed off about a fucking necklace."

They crushed their butts, he clicked open his van doors, and they got in and drove away.

"What, they don't even care if you pay or not?" Ricky asked, checking his sideview mirror.

"Just a Coke and a beer. Think the cops would bother chasing us down? *Car chase through Detroit over $5 check. Drug dealers line the streets, enjoying the entertainment.*"

"You know Detroit, we love a good chase scene." He stopped at a yellow light.

"You could've made it," she said.

"No hurry, now that we've ditched the fuzz," he said.

"How's business?" she asked. "Shouldn't you be rescuing some damsel in distress?"

"More often, it's guys. Purses better than pockets."

It was only three. Ricky wanted to put in a couple more hours at his locksmith shop, but he had his beeper, and most customers were emergencies anyway. He spent a lot of time driving in his van to get people back into their locked cars, locked houses.

"They always seem so relieved and grateful. It's great," he said.

"Too bad you can't get everybody *out*. They need a locksmith for relationships."

"I think they call those 'attorneys.'"

"No, somebody who could make it all simple—adjust the tumblers, cut a new key, then you're out. Gone."

"Well, 'the key to your heart' is not exactly an original phrase."

"So, you're a wordsmith too. A goddamn jack-of-all trades."

"I'm a poet and I know it. You usually don't start getting nasty till after I give you money."

Ricky drove across Eight Mile Road and into Detroit. Hazel leaned back and closed her eyes, breathing heavily through her mouth. The houses around them seemed to sag with resignation at their own impending demise. The weedy vacant lots between the remaining houses created an odd imbalance, as if the houses had been scattered randomly from above like somebody sowing seeds—an old, tainted batch of seeds.

"On the way up, I was thinking about that time I gave you a blow job. Remember that?" Hazel had wedged her wiry frame sideways into the corner of the seat and was looking directly at him.

"No, I don't. . . . Jesus, Hazel. We agreed . . ."

"Did you ever tell the bitch?"

"Shara. What do you think? Is this some kind of blackmail? Jesus—Jesus Christ, Hazel, where have you been?" He pounded the steering wheel.

"I guess I seem doped up," she said, "but I'm not. I just feel like I must seem doped up. There's this lag time between what I do and what I feel later."

Hazel headed south every winter. Slept on the beach, or on couches or floors, or even shared an apartment when things were good, when someone had faith in her. He had no idea from year to year, week to week, what kind of arrangement she had for survival. She never gave him a mailing address. Each summer, she Greyhounded it up from Florida with a battered suitcase of dirty clothes and a story that didn't wash.

Did she seem doped up? Yes, she did. No jobs in Detroit, so she couldn't stay long. Ricky wondered if waitressing was her euphemism for prostitution, but he never asked, not since the one time he had.

"Do you want fries with that?" she'd asked with a forced laugh, not waiting for an answer, her face turning away as if from a cloud of fine, toxic dust.

"She still won't see you," he said, just to explain again as he hit the automatic door lock and they plunged deeper into the half-erased sketch of the city. He wanted to tell her how bad things were with Shara, that it was a terrible time for her to show up. If he wasn't drowning, he was taking on a lot of water, and Hazel looked like she could latch onto him and pull him under for good. She had a desperate glaze to her eyes, even while cutting him down. Her bitterness propped her up, kept her from begging.

He dropped her off at the Triangle Hotel, a three-story brick building on the crumbling edge of downtown—one of those old buildings you assumed hadn't been a hotel in fifty years, but this one apparently took in all comers with cash. Not a triangle in sight. He looked up at the dingy curtains limp in the windows above the Triangle Bar. He winced as he watched her walk through the dented gray metal door, an indecipherable black scrawl of graffiti smeared across it. This too was part of the routine now that she'd ruined things with Shara—Hazel stayed at the worst dump she could find. Who did she think she was punishing? Ricky gave the horn a light tap and pulled away slowly.

"Let's sleep down here tonight," Hazel said.

"I get the couch," he said.

"At least blow up the air mattress for me," she said.

Alone together in their grandparents' tiny box house, they sat sprawled on the ratty couch kept in the basement. It sat in front of an old black-and-white TV that got two and a half stations. Ricky was nearly sixteen, Hazel thirteen. They were talking about sex. Their neighbor Cindee, also sixteen, was pregnant. It was like someone on the street had gotten shot. Adults talked in hushed tones, kept their kids in at night, but it seeped through locked doors, slid up beneath the skin of every teenager on the block: Who was the father? Didn't he use a rubber? What would she do with the baby? Cindee's own father returned from wherever he'd been for three years, seeking vengeance or justice, depending on how many beers he'd had that day.

"How about you? You the daddy?"

"Yeah, right," Ricky said. In fact, he'd had sex with Cindee. She was blazing a trail of bitter rebellion that Hazel was soon to follow. Sex with Cindee was like a drunken brawl. Angry and reckless, she'd pinned him against a tree in the park as if he was that tree.

"But you've done it, right?"

"None of your business."

"If I was going to do it, I—I mean, who wants to get pregnant?"

"If anybody got you pregnant, I'd have to kill him," he said. "You can do shit without getting pregnant."

It was one of the hottest days of a long, hot summer. Even in the damp basement, it was hard to breathe. She went over to the dryer and pulled out one of his T-shirts, then quickly stripped, her back to him, and pulled the shirt over her head. It hung down over her thighs, but rose almost to her hips as she plopped down on the couch again.

"Hey," he started to protest. It was too hot. He stripped to his boxers. When he got up to turn on the TV, an erection poked awkward and obvious against the thin fabric.

Ricky wondered why he'd let Hazel do it. Because no one was looking after them? Because they could? Did other brothers and sisters do that kind of thing, just to experiment? He was older. He should've stopped her. But he didn't. It was the wrong thing. No one from then on could ever stop her from doing the wrong thing.

He remembered the brief, intense pleasure. He'd felt safe and calm down in the silent basement with the only person in the world he trusted. Afterward, she slept on the couch, and he slept on the uninflated air mattress. By the morning, his regret had soaked its imprint into the limp fabric.

After closing up shop, Ricky passed his house, drove a square mile around it, then slowly pulled into the driveway. He was thinking. He was looking for comfort in the square grids of Detroit, the mile roads, how you could never get lost.

"You spying on me?" Shara asked as he unlocked the door and walked in. "I saw you drive by before."

"Why would I be spying on you?" Ricky asked. He walked past her to the fridge, opened it and shut it, taking nothing.

"Why would you drive past your own house?" she asked.

Ricky had no answer. "Why would I be spying on you?" he repeated. He went back to the fridge and pulled out a beer.

Shara was a part-time beautician. She'd had her hours cut due to a big drop in business. Though she had more time on her hands, the house was messier than ever. He couldn't find a clean glass, so he drank from the can.

By mutual agreement, they'd taken the possibility of having kids off the table two years ago, after trying seriously for three. They waited for the pressure and tension and blame to ease up, but it had not eased up, instead morphing into a prickly silence, the subtle sting of resentment. Families were springing up all around them as their old suburban neighborhood in Royal Oak turned over from one generation to the next. They had two empty bedrooms, and it was a shame Hazel couldn't stay in one of them, he thought, even though she had stolen Shara's necklace. A necklace Ricky had bought for their anniversary. Thick, gaudy gold, and Hazel could not resist, though it was worth much less than she'd imagined.

Hazel had arrived in Detroit strung out on crack, and Ricky had been trying his own brand of rehab, which involved locking her in and waiting it out. She disappeared with the necklace and all the cash from Ricky's wallet. It was a betrayal of the first degree, Ricky understood. But it was also a sickness, addiction. And it was his sister, Hazel. And he loved her, his only tenuous link to family. Their parents had both died before they were out of high school—their father of a heart attack when Ricky was nine, and their mother when he was fifteen, of breast cancer.

Ricky and Hazel ended up with their grandparents, who were old and tired, barely able to hold on till the kids were out of high school, out of the house, and on their own. When Hazel got pregnant her senior year, they never knew. Ricky drove her down to an abortion clinic in Toledo. He did not kill the obvious father, her boyfriend, Greg, who had actually gotten the money together to pay for it before disappearing.

After a couple of beers and no sign of dinner on its way, Ricky told Shara, "My sister's in town. I thought you should know. I'll be seeing her from time to time."

"Really?" Shara said. Ricky expected more, a lot more, but she continued watching TV. A reality show about pets.

"She's trying to get her shit together."

"That sister of yours will never get it together," Shara said. She lifted her hand to where a necklace would be and let it rest on her chest. "Though I wish you had some of her . . . you know . . ." Shara waved an arm around in the air as if that explained everything.

Ricky stood waiting, trying not to get sucked into the screen, where two men were arguing about dogs. "You wish I had . . . what?"

"Tired of locks and keys, that's all. We've—look, I've—we need to talk, Rick. With your sister here, maybe it's time."

"Here I am," he said. He sat down in the recliner and leaned forward, his hands together. "I haven't given her any money. I'm waiting to see how she holds up. She says she's straight, but she don't look right. I—would you come and—"

Shara shook her head vigorously and held her hands up as if she was fending off a blow. She got up and left the room. "Just see her!" he shouted, but Shara was gone, and gone in a way he had not anticipated, for she didn't seem to be thinking of Hazel at all. He sat down and watched a dog get voted out of the kennel. He fell asleep and woke to the local news. When he got into bed, Shara was asleep.

The next morning, Hazel showed up at the shop. If she planned to stick around awhile, he'd have to get her a cell phone. Who knew when and where she'd show up with her carelessly wrapped package ready to unravel. The pay phones were disappearing—when he first got his business started, everyone locked out called him from pay phones, found his number in the old frayed yellow pages chained to the booth.

He stopped grinding a key and looked up at Hazel with both expectation and dread. Though deep creases lined the edges of her mouth, veering down toward the jaw line, and her long hair streaked with gray was matted and uncombed, he could still see a hint of the beauty that had the boys circling their grandparents' house in their junker cars, waiting for her to emerge, waiting to offer a ride that she often took because she had no means of transporting herself.

"I'm ready," she said.

"Ready?"

"To have our talk."

"Suddenly everyone wants to talk," he mumbled. Perhaps he'd gotten so used to the gratitude from his customers that he was beginning to resent anyone who did not offer him the same clear uncomplicated thanks. "Tell me something I haven't heard before."

Hazel twirled his rack of key blanks on the counter, and they clinked and rattled against each other. Most of the other girls from their old neighborhood ended up either marrying guys who worked in the factory or working in the factory themselves. It was the badge of a respectable life, but the pin had to go in somewhere to hold it on, and Hazel . . . and Hazel. Ricky just sighed.

"I always liked the smell of this place," she said.

"Smells like work. Must smell exotic to you." He looked around for something to occupy his hands.

"Do you have those pictures from when we were kids?" she asked.

"Back at the house. Those pictures aren't gonna tell you who you are, sister. They'll just make you sad."

"Maybe I need to be sad like that. Start remembering something that matters. I should've stolen those and not the damn necklace."

Ricky hesitated. "Last night, Shara . . ." Then he stopped. "Where can I put money for you so it'll be safe? I can't flush it down the toilet one more time. If you had an address, I could send you a monthly check."

"Do you think I could get back in school? Get a GED or something?"

"Get yourself straight first."

She bit her lip. "I'm tired, Ricky."

"The whole world's tired, babe. You ain't special when it comes to that. You gotta stop thinking of yourself as the center of the universe. I'm out there floating around too, you know."

Hazel pulled herself into him violently, wracking sobs into his chest, wetting his shirt. She went on and on, pummeling him with grief, despair, withdrawal, love—everything she had no words for. He held her until she stopped. This, too, he had seen before.

He let her sit silently in the shop while he worked. She took five dollars from him to go out for coffee, but she never returned. They both knew there was no place to get coffee within miles of the shop, a tiny niche in an old, half-abandoned strip mall in Hazel Park on the edge of Detroit. She didn't know what to do with herself. Any rickety bridge she'd had to the old neighborhood and her friends there had collapsed long ago.

She was the kind of woman the guys snickered about at high school reunions because they were fat and balding and bored with their predictable lives. Ricky unclenched his teeth. He went outside and stood under the overhang to smoke a cigarette and watch the endless April rain. She had left the umbrella he'd handed her on the sidewalk by the door.

Two days later, Shara called him at work to ask him to meet her for lunch. They hadn't spoken since the dog show on TV.

"Meet you for lunch? That's weird, Shara. We're married, why would we need to meet for lunch?" He shook his head and frowned, pushing his cell phone tight against his ear. He'd been grinding keys. He listened to the silence.

He tried to do the subtle work of fitting the tumblers together into a car ignition cylinder, but his hands shook. He watched the clock until noon.

She wanted to meet out by a new development just off the I-75 exit for Rochester Road, far from the comfort of their own neighborhood.

"You think this is funny?" Ricky asked. They sat in a booth in a Ricky Jr.'s restaurant, a lame hamburger chain with sit-down service. Home of the six-dollar burger. Why does the six-dollar hamburger need a home, he wondered, staring at the plastic-coated menu. He couldn't get his head wrapped around what she'd just told him. That she was leaving. "You picked a Ricky Jr.'s for this?"

"Coincidence, Rick. Like how I met Jerry. . . ."

"I don't want to know his name, I don't want to know how you met, I don't want to see him, I don't want to speak to him. Just forget about him. Come home with me and forget about him."

"He's outside—just in case."

Ricky's anger buzzed so intensely that all he could feel was its feedback. He had only ordered coffee. One look at Shara had suggested it would not be a relaxing little lunch. Her hair was pulled back so severely that it looked like her eyes were stretched open. She wore a dress he'd never seen before, and she looked good.

"In case of what?" he raised his voice. He started coughing. He wanted a cigarette. "I want a cigarette," he said. "Let's get out of here. Let's go home."

"He's right out in the parking lot," she emphasized. "He drove me here."

"Where's your car?" Ricky asked. He felt like someone was committing a crime. Was it her, or had he himself already committed some violation, and this was the sentencing?

"At—at Jerry's. I'm not coming home. I'm moving in with him."

"I told you not to say his name. Look, we can talk about adoption again. You're ambushing me here." He spread his sweaty hands, smearing the table. "This is crazy."

"No, *you* look. He's going to take care of me."

"I don't take care of you?" Ricky's voice rose. It soared past territory it had not visited in years. It was exploring the decibels of a virgin anger.

"Don't try anything. He'll take care of you too if necessary."

"Don't threaten me!" The other man, idling, circling somewhere near. Ricky could smell his breath on her.

The waitress stood over them. "Please keep it down, sir, or I'll have to ask you to leave."

"Why will you have to ask me? Can't you just prefer not to?" Ricky looked around for a manager.

"We'd prefer you leave."

"Can't I get a refill?"

"Give me five bucks, I'll give you five more minutes," she whispered under her breath.

"What, is this like sex? Are you like a prostitute selling table time?" Ricky's face was going numb. He thought of Hazel. She'd know how to deal, or at least how to make enough of a scene to give him some satisfaction, however momentary.

The waitress turned to Shara. "Five minutes."

Shara was fumbling with her cell phone, frantically whispering.

"Turn it off," Ricky said. "Tell him to get the hell away from here."

"I don't need permission. He thinks you're going to hurt me."

"Are you trying to provoke me? Are we being recorded?" Ricky wheeled around in the booth.

"You give that sister of yours more money than you ever gave me."

"You keep her out of this. At least I'm not fucking her," he shouted. Everyone in the restaurant turned. "Like you and that man. Fucking!" Ricky pointed vaguely at the window. He saw a red pickup creeping past.

"Okay, that's it," the manager shouted, rushing over to their booth. "If you don't leave right now, I'm calling the police."

"You don't have to call the police, she's got her boyfriend out in the car," Ricky sputtered, rising from his seat and shoving the manager aside, flinging his napkin in the air as he thrust his way out the door. He sprinted wildly down the block and into the land of no sidewalks, his shoes soaking in the lush grass still thick with rain, until he was gasping for breath. He bent down, hands on his knees. His whole body shook.

His van was parked in the Ricky Jr.'s lot, and he'd have to retrieve it. He circled the block, climbed the fence by the dumpster, and slid into his City Locksmith van. For a long time, he sat there idling. No, he'd never fucked his sister.

Change the locks. Lock, stock, and barrel. Lock me up, throw away the key. Lockdown. Lockbox. Ziplock. Lip-lock. Hammerlock. Scissor lock. Locket in my pocket. Combination lock. Picking the lock. Lock up the wimmen 'n' children.

Unchain my heart.

After driving around for hours, accidentally getting caught in rush hour traffic, Ricky ended up in front of the Triangle, where there always seemed to be parking spots any time of night or day, though the few cars in the street were already becoming familiar in their rust and dust, layered sin or cigarette smoke, beer spray or industrial tree sap. The green Chevy. The black SUV. The blue Focus. The gold van. Transportation specials, one and all.

He slipped inside, and everyone turned to face him. He was a stranger who had let the light in.

"I'm looking for my sister, Hazel," Ricky said. He'd never entered the Triangle, always dropping Hazel off in front, waiting till she was inside— safely, he hoped, but he knew she'd resent him following her. Part of their ritual was that he had to pretend she didn't need him.

"Hey, that's the name of a rock band, Sister Hazel," somebody said.

"Nah, it's Brother Turd, that's the name of a band," somebody else said.

"What the fuck kind of name is Sister Hazel? You can't have a Sister Hazel. There ain't no Saint Hazel," somebody else said.

"Like you know your fucking saints," somebody else said.

They'd clearly forgotten him as suddenly as the door closed, sealing them back in the dark smoky cave.

"I'm looking for your sister too, man," a bearded guy on a stool at the end of the bar said, and Ricky braced for a crude joke. But, no, the man was sober and serious.

"That woman owes me some money."

"Is that all?" Ricky said. "She owes everybody money. Get in line behind me."

"You're family, it don't count," the man said, slowly, with a calm menace.

"How much?"

"Twenty."

"Listen, I'll cover it. Here." Ricky handed over a frayed bill. The man nodded and returned to his drink.

Ricky turned to the bartender. "This hotel upstairs, it wouldn't have mailboxes, would it?"

"Right here, my man," the bartender said, extending his hand.

Ricky sighed.

"Who is that asshole?" someone said aloud.

"Says he's Hazel's sister."

"Brother."

"Whatever."

"Just, if you see her, tell her brother is looking for her," Ricky said. "She has my number."

The bartender kept his hand extended. Ricky looked at it. His sister was living upstairs. He dropped a five into the bartender's palm, walked out, and drove home to assess the damage.

When he pulled up his driveway, he began to feel like he was trespassing on his own life. He felt numbed, like he'd stood too close to an exploding firework. Gunshot. Bomb. The gunpowder sting, his ears ringing. Woozy, he climbed the steps onto the porch, grasping the cold iron railing he had installed for safety during the winter, when things froze, melted, then froze again. He noticed the flower baskets swaying in the wind, filled with dirt and the shriveled remains of last summer's flowers. They'd been hanging there all winter. Storm coming on, Ricky thought. He batted one basket with his fist as he made his way to the door.

He got his toolbox out of the van and slid the door closed with a whoosh. He changed the locks, his hands fumbling, screws bouncing off concrete and into the bushes. He got down on his hands and knees with his flashlight to find them. Maybe Jerry would try to break the door down. One way or another, Ricky felt that she'd have to come back, and he wanted her standing on the porch fumbling with the old key, then suddenly realizing.

When he went into their bedroom to collapse, he saw she'd cleaned out her closet. The towels, sheets. Her dresser. She must've had a moving truck pull up to the door. She'd left the bed.

"She left you at a Ricky *Jr.*'s? Fucking cold. I mean, Ricky. That's so fucked up!" Hazel was shouting into the phone, more animated and manic than she'd been since her arrival back in town, and that wasn't a good sign. She'd called in the middle of the night, waking him. He thought it might be Shara calling to say it'd all been a mistake. He had worked hard to build up his business, buy a nice house in a good neighborhood. He imagined what his neighbors must've been thinking as Shara directed the movers to hurry up. Would he take her back? He'd already changed the locks. But on the phone it was Hazel, not Shara.

"Where are you?" Ricky shouted. "Did you get my message?" Either a bar or a loud party blared in the background.

"What message?" Her voice was the liquid slur of the almighty high.

"I left you a message. At the hotel."

"I can't go back there. I need . . ." Her voice lowered to a loud whisper. "I need . . ." then her voice rose again, "a Ricky Jr.'s!"

"Where are you?" he repeated.

"I'm—I—"

"Hazel, can you ask somebody where you are? Can I talk to someone there?"

Ricky heard a fumbling as the phone dropped, then a man's voice on the line.

"Hey, you know this lady? You gotta get her outta here. She's all fucked up. She won't leave."

Ricky wrote down the address, threw on some clothes, and drove off. He found the low brick building on a street littered with long dark stretches of vacant lots. He didn't want to slow down, much less stop.

Inside, she was passed out on the floor wearing only a faded blue bra and the torn black jeans that she'd been wearing every time he'd seen her since she'd returned.

"Where's her shirt?" Ricky shouted, but no one paid him or Hazel any mind. A live band rattled the windows with fury. He took off his jacket, slid her arms into the sleeves, and zipped it up. He gently roused her and led her to the car as the sky grayed toward dawn.

He drove Hazel back to his house and carried her out of the car in his arms. She was as light as a child, though she stunk with all smells adult and sour. He leaned her gently against the bricks while he unlocked the door with his new key. It was a little tight, but he knew time would smooth it out, round off the rough edges.

He hoisted her back up, and she threw her arms loosely around his neck. Someone looking at them from far away might have thought it was a father carrying his sleepy daughter home, or a husband carrying his new wife across the threshold. The bright, rising sun could force a squint to make any good thing possible. Then he kicked the door shut behind them.

SEPARATED AT BIRTH

DARKNESS BOUNCED OFF THE INSIDES OF THE ALUMINUM ROWBOAT turned upside down in the muddy waters of Tea Lake. Todd felt the warm mist of Angie's breath touch his face. They stood close in cool dark water. His feet sank in the muck. Angie's wide eyes seemed to emit light in that false darkness. Alone there, capsized, all things were possible. Could they be in love?

"When are you going to kiss me, by the way, you big glug?" Angie asked.

They both laughed, their voices echoing off aluminum. He blew bubbles at her. They both got the joke. They always got each other's jokes. They liked the same music—singer-songwriters with lyrics deep and inscrutable. Bob Dylan. None of their friends liked Dylan—that ugly old guy with the horrible voice. Not even their parents liked Dylan anymore, and that made it even better. Their parents, despite vague nostalgic trappings of counterculture—Todd's father's ponytail, Angie's mother's penchant for going braless on vacation—seemed like top-forty oldies when it came down to it. A little too young for Vietnam, so they hadn't had to think very hard about it.

Friends from college—the University of Michigan—their parents had attended the annual Hash Bash and every home football game. They'd started going on vacation together in northern Michigan before either of their children was born. Todd and Angie were fourteen now. These annual summer trips had always been a part of the rhythm of their lives. The weeks at Carl's Friendly Kabins on Tea Lake were like spikes pounded in to secure the borders of every year.

"If we kissed," Todd whispered, just for the drama of it. "What would happen then?"

"More kissing, perhaps," Angie said. She floated away and blew him kisses from the bow of the overturned boat. It would have been easy to glide through the dark water and take her in his arms, but he'd never taken any girl in his arms before, and Angie was scaring him a bit with her aggressive flirting, something new since last summer.

"*More* kissing?" His voice squeaked a little. Kissing Angie had a safe place in his late-night fantasies. He wasn't sure he wanted those kisses to emerge into the world, even their private world beneath a rowboat where they were both invisible and on display. Nearly everyone living on the small lake could see the overturned boat near shore. No one would think they were drowning, in danger, but they were. At least, Todd felt he was, though he thought that might be good.

Every sound seemed both echoed and muted. When he blurted out "I love you," she said, "What?" even though she'd heard him clearly, just to feel those words penetrate her cool, damp skin again. Oh, the beautiful weight of them. She closed her eyes and treaded water. She wanted everything to remain in place. The happy ending, the curtain falling. The applause.

"I love you," he gurgled in the water, then took a deep dive and swam out beneath the boat. He broke the surface and was hit by the bold, sharp sun glinting off the hull. He gently knocked on the side.

"What?" she said again.

"Are you in there?" he asked.

"Nothing in here but us fishies," she said.

"One fish, two fish, red fish, blue fish," he said. "And by the way . . ." He thought it'd be easier not having to look at her as he asked. The bright glare forced him to squint. "By the way, what do you think of that?"

"What?" she wanted to ask again, but she knew. "I just asked you to kiss me, so how do you think I think?"

"If wishes were fishes we'd all be dishes. . . . I mean, not like the usual—that kiddie stuff our parents think is cute."

"Like the unusual? Why don't you swim back under here?" she asked. "I don't like talking through boats."

Todd took another deep breath and dove. He pulled himself under the boat with long breaststrokes and quickly found her thin legs planted in the muck. He followed them upward and emerged inches from her face. He planted a kiss on her lips, and she grabbed the back of his short hair and pulled him down to kiss him harder.

Maybe the curtain's not coming down, it's just going up, she thought. It was Tuesday. Nondescript Tuesday, when the week seemed neither new nor about to end.

They were born three months apart in 1986. It was the big 2000. Year zero. Not double 0 or triple 0. Just 0. Change your clocks, change your locks. They'd spent New Year's together at Angie's parents' condo in Seven Springs, the ski resort outside of Pittsburgh, where the Rolands, Angie's family, lived.

Todd's family, the Tweedys, lived in West Bloomfield, where his father, Robert, worked as an attorney. Their families spent every New Year's together at the condo. It was a tight squeeze. Up until two years ago, Todd and Angie had slept together on the foldout couch. Even then, it wasn't their parents who suggested Todd move to a sleeping bag on the floor. It was Todd—Angie was developing breasts, he was having wet dreams—who thought it was too weird, though he still slept within whispering distance of Angie. Whispering had been excitement enough only months ago.

The two couples were very close. Todd's relatives in Michigan seemed distant in comparison. His aunts and uncles seemed tight with each other, and with Todd's grandparents, but not with his parents. Even though they all lived within an hour of each other, spread around the suburbs of Detroit, he never saw his father's side of the family except for an annual Christmas visit. His mother, Jen, had no side to speak of—her parents both dead, and she was an only child.

Angie had family in Pittsburgh, though there was often some feud brewing that she filled Todd in on. Her father worked in the family business, a small chain of hardware stores, and everything turned on money—no one trusted anyone. They kept track of how much they spent on each other's Christmas presents. "It's sick," she told Todd. "We can't ever get like that." The only one she felt close to was a sickly grandmother who wrote her letters as if she were an adult and sent her money on her birthday from her Arizona hideout.

When they talked about the future, Angie was a dancer and Todd made movies. When they were together, they sang a lot, but they'd stopped singing in front of their parents. At Seven Springs, they stood in their boots in deep snow and sang to the stars. Todd and Angie liked to get cold and numb, then go back inside and curl up by the fire on big pillows in the living room while their parents mixed drinks and took them down into the basement den.

The four of them—Jen and Robert, his parents, and Tricia and Gene, her parents—had nicknames for each other. They spoke in a code that Todd and Angie had given up trying to decipher long ago. They were more interested in interpreting Dylan lyrics than the odd, flirty exchanges between Jen-Jen and Bobbo, Cha-Cha and Geno. They had their own code, though no one had ever been interested in deciphering it.

"We're just little accessories," Angie said as they dried off in the old bouncy metal chairs on the small splintery dock that extended into the lake.

"We're not so little anymore." He scratched at rust on his armrest. "Carl's really been letting this place go," he said.

"I think it was always a pit," she said. "We just didn't notice before. We're also not so cute anymore."

"Speak for yourself. I am cute as hell." He brushed the hair out of his eyes and smiled, still giddy with kisses.

"I mean 'kid cute.' Hold-your-mommy-and-daddy's-hand-and-swing-between-them cute."

"They love us. At least, that's what they say all the time."

"Too much, they say it," Angie said. "They love themselves. They love each other." She closed her eyes and tilted her chin up toward the sun.

"That sounds a little harsh. They leave us alone now."

"They've always left us alone. They never wanted to know where we were going. Not like other parents. We could've drowned in this lake a hundred times."

"They got us the best swimming lessons."

"Ah, Marina . . ." Angie smiled suddenly. "We should try and find her."

"Wouldn't it be depressing? She's probably got like six kids by now and bagging groceries down at the IGA."

"We went to the IGA. She's not there."

"That could be a good thing," Todd said. "Wouldn't it be great if she was teaching swimming again?"

"Our parents can afford better than this. Do they come here because they think we love it or something?"

"Do we love it?"

"I don't think so."

Todd remembered Marina's powerful, effortless strokes, her broad shoulders, rippling muscles. Her deep tan and sun-bleached hair. A lake girl. A fish. She'd given them swimming lessons the summer they were ten. She was fifteen then and had a boyfriend, Al, a swimmer too. They swam for the school team and lifeguarded in the summer, squeezing in some lessons on the side. Todd and Angie thought they were the perfect couple. Todd's first crush was on Marina, and Angie's was on Al. When they returned the summer following their lessons, they found out she'd gotten pregnant, and they'd had an imperfect wedding, then both dropped out of school, and Al took a job down at the lumberyard where his dad worked. All this, according to Carl Metrovich, the owner of Carl's Friendly—Carl's Friendly Kabins, but half the sign had been cut off by a chainsaw or drunk driver or snow plow one year, and Carl had never fixed it. They bugged Carl when they were bored, and he told them things their parents never would. Todd and Angie called him Carl Metallica. He was in his early fifties and had more tattoos than anyone in Pittsburgh or West Bloomfield, or any other burgh or field they'd passed through. An old motorcycle dude, Carl had acquired the resort in a complicated transaction that may have involved drugs. Carl was always telling them, "Don't do drugs." Usually adding a phrase under his breath like, "You might not get out alive like I did." Or, "They'll bite you on the ass someday." Or, "Your body is a temple."

Todd always wanted to tell Carl that if his body was a temple, then he needed to do some repair work, but Carl scared them both a little. When he was calm, he seemed almost too calm, and when he was agitated, they didn't go near him.

How their parents had ever found Carl's Friendly, a tiny speck on one of the hundreds of small inland lakes in Michigan, was something that was encoded and joked about with Carl. Carl had one bad eye that wouldn't stay open—a relic of some bar fight—so it always looked like he was winking at you. "At least I never killed nobody," Carl would occasionally mutter, apropos of nothing. He spent his summers at the Kabins and worked winters as a bouncer/bartender at Boyne Mountain, a small ski resort nearby—to "level things out," he told them, though Carl always seemed askew, far from level, more darkness than light.

When they asked Carl about Marina and Al, he made a face and said they didn't want to know. They'd both been hit hard by the premature tying of that knot. They couldn't let it go. They swam alone now, and no one watched them or taught them a thing.

"For kids around here, the summers they're fifteen, sixteen, that's like the highlight of their lives. You kids are from la-la land, where kids finish high school and their parents take care of them when they get in trouble. Around here . . ." he paused, "rules are different."

This summer, Carl had some news, and it wasn't good. Al had left Marina, left her with their *three* kids. "Al hit the road on a solo journey," he said. Carl was walking around the dock with a hammer, but he wasn't hammering anything. He looked like he was taking notes on what he'd have to hammer once he no longer had a choice about hammering or not.

"Where's Marina?"

"She's in a place you youngsters don't want to go."

"Prison?"

"Prison'd be a good thing for her right now."

That shut them up. Carl smacked the hammer into his palm and walked back into the woods.

"I'm depressed," Angie said. "Let's get some drugs." They swung their held hands in the small space between deck chairs. Angie was nearly out of control. Todd banged his elbow against the armrest and let go of her hand.

"I've got vitamins and aspirin."

"Let's take one of each."

"How could Al leave Marina?" Todd felt betrayed, the neat fantasy future of their early gods drowned in the murky lake.

"It's like an after-school special."

"What's the moral, then? Sounds more like a soap opera. No moral, just drama."

"Poor Marina."

"Don't they have, like, birth control up here?"

"How come we're both only-childs?"

"Shouldn't it be 'only children'?"

"How come we're flying solo on this thing?"

"This thing?"

"Life."

"But we have each other."

"That's what my parents said when I asked them."

"You asked them?"

"Sure."

"Isn't that a little bit of pressure on us? We just went through puberty and we're supposed to be each other's legal guardians or some shit. . . . So, I'm not enough, then?"

"You're more than enough. You're too much, Mr. Todd."

"Let's never have nicknames for each other, okay? Hey, isn't 'Angie' a nickname?"

"It's a diminutive. It's a shortening. It's not some weird baby talk thing like 'Bobbo' and 'Geno.'"

"'Ang.' That sounds like the name of a tool. 'Hand me that ang, will ya.

The thingamabob is stuck. Just needs a coupla yanks with a good ang, and it'll loosen right up.'"

"You want a couple of yanks, huh?" Angie pulled on his arm, his nose, his ears, and they rolled onto the scratchy grass at the edge of the dock. Todd laughed so hard his eyes were watering, and he had to run away to catch his breath and hide his erection.

"What's the matter, can't take it, huh?"

"I like 'Todd.' It's unnicknameable."

"Toddy. The Toddster. Todd-o-rama. Todd the Bod."

Todd struck a bodybuilder pose. They broke into laughter again. Todd was scrawny, almost skeletal, though he ate constantly. His ribs were visible like faded war paint on his chest. They were both very thin, and people often mistook them for brother and sister, or maybe that was just a perception their parents encouraged.

"Marina and Al," Todd said. "Let's get out of here before I forget how to swim."

Together they ran up the dirt path from Carl's to US 30, the main road cutting through the thick woods in the northwest corner of the Lower Peninsula. They wanted to run farther, so they turned and ran back the other way. They had no idea where their parents were. They stopped and made peanut butter and jelly sandwiches at Todd's cabin and ate them with grapes on the screened-in porch. They played Monopoly.

They were all seated in a circle around the evening campfire. Carl had five cabins, and their families had two of them. The other three cabins were occupied by (1) a set of grandparents who were supposed to have grandchildren with them but did not, (2) an older man with a much younger woman, and (3) a couple of friends of Carl's who claimed to be tattoo artists, and while their flabby displays of patterned skin seemed to bear this out, with Carl's friends there always seemed to be another story, one that Todd and Angie never could quite figure out, and one their parents didn't think twice about. The others all seemed to stay away from the lake and go to bed early, except for the grandparents, who politely exited the bonfire shortly after dark each night.

It was baked potato night, as opposed to hobo pie night or popcorn night. Every night was marshmallow night. Without campfires, Carl's would be a grim place, sticky with mosquitoes and the rot of wood where the sun never hit.

Carl let Bobbo and Geno get the fire started. It was an honor bestowed only on long-term Friendlys, he claimed. The men carefully made their little tepees of sticks, then poured charcoal lighter over the whole thing to be sure. Bobbo lit the one match, tossed it on, and Carl nodded approval before disappearing. Carl came and went like an over-caffeinated buffalo. He couldn't stand still. He couldn't sit.

Todd and Angie squeezed together on one of the metal chairs. Carl had painted them a bright red that when damp turned tacky all over again. Their skinny torsos fit neatly into the one chair with room to spare. Their parents never cared how close they sat or stood or walked or slept.

The baked potatoes were buried in aluminum foil in the glowing coals. Todd could smell the thick, sweet burn of them. The paper plates and butter and salt and pepper sat on the picnic table. All seemed right with the world.

Their parents sat clustered in a semicircle on the other side of the fire like a hastily summoned jury or a drunken string quartet. The smoke blew at Angie and Todd—they held their breaths and closed their eyes and turned their faces toward each other, waiting for the wind to change direction, but it would not change.

"Let's blow this pop stand," Angie whispered. "My eyes are burning with boredom."

"But the potatoes," Todd whispered back. "Ve must eat da potatoes."

"What kind of accent is that?"

"A hungry accent . . . a Hungry-arian accent. Ha!"

"Uncle Bobbo, can we see if they're done yet?" Angie turned to Todd's father. They'd been instructed since birth to call each other's parents Aunt and Uncle.

"I'm timing them, sweetheart. Five more minutes. Why don't you kids roast marshmallows?"

"We don't do marshmallows anymore," Angie said. "Too sticky," they said in unison, then "Jinx!" at each other. Todd laughed, but he wanted marshmallows too. He had sharpened sticks for himself and Angie. He wanted everything else to freeze while he and Angie emerged from the still life, 3D and in love.

"Remember that time with the marshmallows?" Cha-Cha asked. The adults snickered. Angie sighed and put her hand firmly on Todd's thigh and squeezed. He jumped.

"Twixt and 'tween," Geno said.

"Holy Moly," Bobbo said.

"Eat it," Jen-Jen said and stuck out her tongue.

The adults erupted into laughter. The empty beer bottles glistened brown and flickered in flame light.

"I think they're done," Todd said. "I'll test one." He grabbed the long-handled fork leaning against the weathered picnic table, stabbed a ball of aluminum foil, and lifted it out of the fire and onto the table.

"I said five minutes," Bobbo said.

"They're teenagers now," Cha-Cha said.

"What's that mean?" Geno asked.

"What it's always meant," Jen-Jen said. "They're contrarians."

"They stay up too late and sleep in too late," Cha-Cha said.

"Messing with the system," Bobbo mumbled.

Todd carefully peeled away the aluminum foil, took a fork and split the charred potato skin, steam rising in the light from one of Carl's tiki torches.

"Done," Angie whispered. They were used to being both outnumbered and ignored, but recently their parents seemed irritated with them, particularly at night. Angie felt like they were being silently scrutinized for signs of illness; in the past, her parents had seemed this attentive only when she was sick.

Todd pulled out the rest of the potatoes, flinging them into the bowl on the table. He and Angie tossed theirs on paper plates and slipped off onto the path back to the cabins, leaving their parents in the process of distributing another round of beers. They stopped at Angie's cabin and sat at the sticky picnic table inside the screened-in porch, eating their potatoes. "Uncle Geno. dyed his hair," Todd said, swallowing a mouthful of hot potato.

"No shit," Angie said.

She had taken up swearing. Todd smiled. He had too. It felt good to roll the words around in his mouth, feel their toxic fizz, then spit them out.

"Just before we left," she added, running a hand through Todd's neat blond hair. "The car smelled like it. My mom was mad."

"It looks a little purple-brownish. I don't think that's his natural color."

"Purple brownish—that was the color he picked. . . . Let's run away and get married."

"Like Al and Marina?"

"You're giving me your skins, right? No, this is Pretendville—we live happily ever after."

"Sorry, I forgot. Do we have any kids?"

"That would require us to, you know . . ." She nudged him and winked broadly.

"Have jobs?"

"Yeah, *jobs*. Nudge nudge, wink wink."

"Here are your skins." Todd dropped them into her cupped hands and ran out the screen door and into the clearing in the middle of the circle of dark, quiet cabins. The tiny floodlight above the fish-cleaning shack barely dented the darkness. He waited impatiently for Angie to emerge. He wanted to run and run and run through the night.

"Angie," he said simply as she stepped into the clearing, licking her fingers.

"Good skins," she said. "Thanks." She threw her aluminum-foil ball at him. He picked it up and tossed it in the stinky garbage can next to the fish shack, then ran back to her.

"Something fishy around here. Nobody's been fishing, but it smells fishy."

"Let's go for a walk," she said. "A brisk walk."

"Carl needs to expand the track here. It's just for sprinters, and me and you, we're long-distance runners. We're fucking marathoners."

"I think every book should be titled *Before and After*," she said and stepped up close to him. "We have just entered the 'After' part. Watch your step."

"After? We're just getting started."

"Don't you think a first kiss deserves an After?"

"First kiss is what they call a Prelude."

"You're just such a smarty pants, I can't stand it," and she reached up and kissed him again, sloppy, with a lot of tongue.

He pulled back. "Tongue—that was cool! Now I really need to go for a brisk *run!*" He took off down the narrow path toward the road. She ran after him.

The sky was clear enough to see all the stars they couldn't see back in their cities. "Baby, I'm seeing stars," she shouted and laughed, quickly catching up to him, squeezing past. She ran out of the resort and down onto US 30, Todd following, until their lungs burned. They stopped to watch four deer cross the road silently in front of them.

"We just need to change the rules, and we'll have more room to run," she said, wrapping her arms around his thin chest. "Did I tell you I love you too?" she said suddenly. "All the books give contradictory advice on this point. Who says it first, then what do you say back, and then, how often do you say it after that?"

"I—I love you," he said, again. It was harder this time—he wasn't sure why.

"I love you too, Todd. Let's burn the books and keep each other warm." It was time for them to kiss again, but they didn't. They crouched in the middle of the road and leaned their sweaty foreheads together.

"I'm saying a prayer," he whispered.

She almost laughed, expecting him to make a joke, but he didn't, and she said nothing, making a silent wish that could've been a prayer. When they heard a car in the distance, they hopped like frogs onto the gravel shoulder, then stood and walked back to Carl's.

"Do you think our parents will notice?" Todd asked.

"Let's make out at dinner tomorrow and see," Angie said.

"I'm not sure we've made out yet. I thought that meant like kissing for a half hour or something. I think we need more practice before auditioning for the folks. . . . Shouldn't we love our parents more?" Todd asked. "We're always dissing them."

"Like Jen-Jen said, we're teenagers, that's what we're supposed to do. When we get older, we're supposed to start liking them again."

"When I'm with my cousins, they—I don't know, maybe it's the whole only-child thing, but they. . . . I feel like I need to fake it, pretend we're this tight little family to keep up with them. They seem like they still love their parents, and some of them are teenagers and everything."

"You just don't see them often enough."

"I want to love my parents more, I do," Todd said. "Why did they have us anyway?"

"You're asking me? You complaining now, huh, big boy?" She put her warm wet lips against his, and he felt a shiver of pleasure and pulled her tight.

They'd snuck out at 3 A.M. and were sitting at the picnic table on the dock watching the water slosh softly against shore. The tiki torches had long been extinguished, and only floodlights on distant docks broke up their night on earth. Above them, the stars dazzled.

"Remember the Naganos?" Angie asked. "From a couple of years ago?" She held Todd's hand. They were getting used to it, spreading their fingers to accommodate each other. They had held hands for years, but always in motion—crossing streets, parking lots, entering and exiting grocery stores, or wandering through Kennywood, the amusement park in Pittsburgh that was an annual outing for their families, another calendared ritual that they shared. They were learning to hold hands all over again, thinking about it— not too tight, but tight enough. To squeeze at both random and designated moments.

"I remember that girl, Sally. Long, beautiful black hair. She tied it up to go swimming, then untied it and let it fan out around her when she lay on the dock."

"What?"

"We were eleven. You can't be jealous?"

"I liked her hair too. *She* liked her hair. She spent half the day brushing it."

"Hair like that . . ." Todd said.

"Didn't they leave in a huff about something?"

"Yeah, it was so anti–Carl's Friendly . . ."

"But we never found out why."

"I remember when they sped off, a big cloud of dust, and Carl throwing his arms in the air like, 'C'mon, people, let's be reasonable here.'"

"Or, he might've said, 'Fuck you, people, good riddens.'"

"Carl has recessive motorcycle-gang genes."

"They were nice people, the Naganos. Quiet, smiling, polite."

"They even bowed. What the hell were they doing here? It was like they were shipwrecked, stranded." Todd looked around and took in the cool, clear stillness around them.

"Like they'd gotten on the wrong plane."

"And landed in upside-down land."

"Their camera was useless here."

"Sally seemed so calm."

"Protected by her hair."

"What happened?" they said together.

"Sometimes I don't know when you're talking and when I'm talking," Todd said.

"Just look at my lips. When they're moving, that's me talking," Angie giggled. "This place used to be so big," she sighed. "Now it's a tea cup full of water, and I feel like I'm stuck at this little table in this stuffy room."

Todd gave her a look.

"I mean us, us together. Now that we're—together—it seems a lot smaller. That's why we're up in the middle of the night. We've excused ourselves from the big table. We've snuck away," she whispered.

"Look at the stars," Todd whispered back.

"They seem super close tonight," she said. She pulled her to him, and they began auditioning for the moon.

Todd's lips were sore. They'd spent a good hour kissing. His tongue hurt too. He had slipped a hand into the back of Angie's jeans and felt the soft elastic band of her panties, but he didn't feel the urgency to push further. Kissing seemed plenty. He was sleepy and cold. "Three more days," he said.

"That gives me a chill," Angie said. "Let's go back before the werewolves come out."

"How many nights is the moon full? I feel like I should know that," Todd said. Together, they lifted off the bench, briefly disentangling their hands, only to immediately join them again. They headed back to the cabins. Todd felt like they were like deer in their gentle silence, their alertness. He didn't think he'd be able to sleep, but he needed to lie down and let his body absorb the kisses and be nourished. He quickly pulled open the screen door to his cabin—he knew it squeaked when you pulled slowly—and he saw a body back away from the door. Angie's father, Bobbo.

"Shhh," he whispered to Todd. "Thought I left something here." He quickly stepped around Todd and slipped out the door. Todd held it so it wouldn't smack against its frame and wake his parents. Bobbo held nothing in his hands. Todd watched him scurry over the dirt road between cabins wearing only a pair of plaid boxers.

He passed his parents' closed door and headed to his room in the back of the cabin. Their room had a window air conditioner, and it hummed loudly, though Todd's room, with the window open, was comfortable, even cool.

He lay there trying to hold onto the fullness of Angie, the newness, the nowness. His eyes were closed, but he felt wide open. He wanted to sing, or at least hum away the strange phantom of her father. He was just drifting off when he heard the screen door creak open and shut, then his parents' door open and shut. He pulled the thin sheet up tight around him.

In the morning, he rose early, but his mother was already up, cooking pancakes. Todd stared at the mirage. His mother never made pancakes or cooked anything for breakfast.

"Good morning, dear," his mother said, her voice shrill and weighted. "I'm making breakfast today!" The pancakes were smoking, burning. The griddle was too hot. Todd knew how to make pancakes. He slipped past her.

"Wait, dear!" his mother commanded. She hadn't even made coffee, Todd noticed.

"Lower the heat," he said. "I left something on the dock." He hurried out and across to Angie's, where he scratched on her window screen until she pushed her face against it, flattening her rumpled hair.

"What?" she said. She looked at his face. "Five minutes. End of the dock."

"Last night, when I was walking into my cabin," Todd began. His feet dangled off the dock, his sneakers on top of the water, slapping against it as if he was walking on the stillness. Angie was barefoot, her legs pulled up beneath her.

"I walked into *your dad* coming out. Then later, I heard somebody come *in.*"

"Todd! Todd! Your pancakes are getting cold!" His mother had clattered onto the deck in her short robe and his father's dress shoes.

"Should I drown now?" he asked glumly. "Or wait till I have my pancakes?"

Angie simply stared down into the water.

"Guess I'll have the pancakes," he said. "They'll help weigh me down."

She reached up and squeezed his hand hard.

"Todd!" his mother shouted again. He rose slowly, sure that whatever she'd made had turned to ash.

That afternoon, they escaped under the rowboat, but Todd felt trapped, claustrophobic. "Everyone's acting like they wet the bed or something last night, and they're worried I'm gonna tell. What's it like at your cabin?"

She said nothing.

"Your father half naked in my cabin in the middle of the night. Doesn't that seem strange to you?"

Still, she was silent.

A steady rain bounced off the boat like rolling dice.

"Doesn't it? And then the pancakes. All black, but gooey in the middle, and my mom spilling her coffee and wearing my dad's shoes and not thinking anything is funny."

Angie began to cry, sobbing so loud that Todd became frightened. He pulled her to him, and her hot tears landed on his bony, wet shoulder until he cried too. Her body was wracked with it. She tried to speak but could not. He had simply thought it strange, another odd encoded occurrence involving their odd encoded parents.

Todd pulled away and ducked out into the overcast light to see if anyone was observing the overturned boat, drawn by the sounds a caught fish might make, if fish could make noise. Todd thought a whole lot less people would fish if they could hear the pain of the hook. It was their silent if stubborn surrender that made it easy, doable—sport.

He ducked back under. Angie was slowly calming. "You have to stay with me," she said firmly. Whatever it was, it was serious, beyond them, out in a far world where the language was untranslatable, the currency without denominations.

"They must be," she began with a deep shuddering breath. "I think they're—they're switching—swapping."

"Swapping? Like baseball cards?" Todd asked. "What?" he shouted and raised his arms out of the water and pushed up on the boat, but he could not hold it, and it splashed back down.

"Twice. Once at the condo, and once here last year, I . . ." she faltered again.

He felt a strange rush of hatred for Angie but held it in.

"Maybe it's something else. I mean, you know how they are," Todd cried.

He remembered them dancing together at the mountain condo, the four adults, drunk, silly, and how they'd switched partners, grinding into each other in the dining room, the table pushed aside, as he and Angie silently watched a video in the living room. He remembered his mother—did he really remember this?—feeding Bobbo eggs in the kitchen one morning when his own father was nowhere to be found.

He couldn't breathe. He needed to be out in the rain, not sheltered from it. "Let's swim out to the island," he said. A small strip of land with a few trees and scraggly bushes sat in the middle of the lake. It had been an accomplishment to swim that far. A dare, and they had made it the summer after lessons and every summer since. Swimming without a net, they called it.

"No," she said. "Stay. Make me think it's not true. I still think it's true. It makes me want to puke. I knew, but I didn't know. You tell me this, and I can't un-know it."

She seemed slight in her sleek one-piece suit. A minnow.

"It's true," Todd said, and as soon as he said it, he was certain.

When he was younger, two things twisted him into cold sweats: the idea of his parents dying and the idea of living forever. He couldn't grasp the concept of things never ending, but he didn't want things to end either. He felt that way now. As if all connection to a system for the world had been severed, and he was free-floating, losing oxygen and clarity and whatever faith he had. Like a spacewalk gone bad, and in all that space he struggled to find Angie.

"We have to run away," she said, and he nodded, though he doubted she could see in the dim half-light beneath the boat.

"When?"

"Yesterday. I can't face them."

"We didn't do anything wrong. Why should we run away? How can *they* face *us?* How long—are they really even our parents?"

"How much money do you have? Where can we get money? Where can we go? Should we tell someone?" The questions spilled from her. He had to dive out from under the boat and hope she'd follow.

He waited, but she remained beneath it. "They need to be locked up!" Todd shouted, and now it was he who broke into angry sobs, punching at the still water.

"You love one person . . ." she said firmly from the hollow darkness, "like that. That's the way the world's supposed to work."

"They should die for this," Todd said. He couldn't think of anything extreme enough to say, to stop the sinking into the bottomless muck of the—it was really a large pond, not a lake. "This—this ruins our lives, do you understand?" He wanted or needed no answer.

The books she'd read said nothing of this. People broke up, they went with other people, they moved on. They didn't do this. She swam out into the light, and together they flipped the boat over. They each picked up an oar from shore and pushed off. In sync, they pulled hard, and the boat rode high in the water as they rowed to nowhere.

Darkness hit quickly, the gray ceding to black. They'd beached on the island and stared back at the cabins like an enemy encampment that they had to either flee from or attack. All afternoon they'd rowed in circles. They'd gotten sunburned, despite the overcast skies. They now sat anchored on the far side of the lake as if they were fishing. Before and After. Todd studied Angie's face, but when she looked him directly in the eye, he had to turn away. Pretendville had either disappeared completely or taken on an entirely different location.

He thought of the unmarked videos in his parents' bedroom he'd stumbled onto one day when bored and alone. What would he have seen if he'd pushed *play?* What would he have seen of the parents who never took photographs, who insisted memories were always better?

Angie ached with pain and hunger. When they were younger, at least they packed snacks when they ran away. But for her, this was just an evasive maneuver, a stalling tactic, a smoke signal to be followed up by substance. Her father, his mother. Her mother, his father. She held onto the boat's hard bench. They hadn't even brought float cushions to sit on.

They heard a motor approaching, and soon Carl was pulling up next to them in the small cabin cruiser he used to take people fishing.

"Getting any nibbles?" he asked. "Your parents—both of you—are worried sick and worried mad. You best make up a good story by the time I get done pulling your skinny little asses back in. Unless you want to row in the dark while I drive circles around you. Pull up your anchor and give it to me."

Todd and Angie hesitated, numb and sunburn-chilled. They'd made a plan. Two plans. Three plans, four. But they had no plan. How could they run away and survive? Where? How could they punish their parents? How could they make sure *they* stayed together? Any plan could backfire. They could be separated. He could end up living with relatives in Detroit. She could end up in Arizona with her grandmother. Or—could their parents really try to keep them, go on as if their lives didn't revolve around this *system* of deceit? Could they stuff the cat back in the bag without killing it?

Though the line where lake met shore had disappeared, Todd had begun to see the mirages for what they were. He and Angie were decoys that kept the illusion of normalcy alive: it was their "cute kids" that brought their parents together so much. "You were right about everything," he whispered to her as he moved to the back of the boat. "Props." Todd pulled up the wet anchor and swung it onto the deck of Carl's boat.

"You kids want to tell Carl what you're doing out here? I seen you two making out the other night."

They looked at each other. Caught escaping the big tea party by the Mad Hatter.

Carl waited.

"We saw something ourselves," Angie said. Carl's boat was too big for the small lake. It sputtered loudly as he continued to wait.

"You're not gonna do something to mess up old Carl's Friendly, are ya? . . . Like drowning. That'd really mess up my business," he said. "Heh heh."

"We're both excellent swimmers, as you know," Todd said fiercely.

"Yeah, well, so were Romeo and Juliet," he said. "Don't go playing kid detectives on me, lovebirds. This ain't just about your folks."

"What about the Naganos?" Todd blurted out.

"The Whattos?"

"That Japanese family—three years ago."

Carl stroked his chin as if he still had the biker beard, though he was currently clean shaven. "Just a problem in translation. You kids ask too many questions. You should be thinking up answers."

He revved his engine. The rope tightened, then both boats chugged off across the lake, past the island, and pulled in next to the little dock, where the campfire burned a little too bright. Todd could make out four frightened, frightening faces through the flames, and the strange grandparents off to the side.

"Everybody's got traditions," Carl said, tying up his boat. "Your parents have traditions. Carl's has traditions. You've gotta respect traditions. That's all I'm gonna say."

"*What* were you two *doing* out there?" Cha-Cha asked as they trudged down the dock to the fire pit, heads lowered. Her voice a brittle shriek hollowed out by anger and terror.

"Thought I left something out there," Todd said, looking directly at Bobbo.

"Ah, shit," Bobbo mumbled softly.

"Captain Carl says you two were out here making kissy-face the other night," Geno said.

"No, actually, we were out here fucking on the dock," Angie said. She glared at the grim-faced grandparents. They quickly got up and started back toward the cabins.

"I bet you're not even grandparents. That's just some story. Who are you really?" Todd shouted.

"That's enough," Carl barked. "Take family business inside." He reached for Angie and Todd as the men rose from their seats and moved toward them.

"What are you gonna do, take us prisoner?" Todd continued to shout. "You buncha perverts!" He shivered and shook off Carl's meaty hand. He wanted to run—none of them could catch either of them, but then . . . then, where? "Leave us alone," he yelled. "Like you used to do. Go do your thing, all of you. Just go do it. Leave us out of it. We'll sleep in the fish shack. It won't stink as bad as it does right here." He looked at Angie, hoping for her strength, her sharp edge to cut them down.

"Shut up, Todd," his father said. "Go on up to the cabin *now.*"

Angie was shriveling before his eyes. Even her hand seemed smaller in his. Everyone stood. Carl hung back at the fire and watched them all trudge up to the cabins.

Carl's wasn't much to look at, but it was remote, private. Carl ran a tight ship so everything else could be loose. Loosey-goosey. Maybe the broken-off "Kabins" was a secret sign for swingers. Todd was dizzy with hunger and cold and lies and—his whole life. Angie let go of his hand, and they were separated into the darkness, Todd with his parents, Angie with hers.

"We'll stop," his mother said as soon as the screen slammed behind them. "We should have stopped years ago. It was just . . ."

"You wouldn't understand," his father said evenly. He spread his hands out as if gently patting the top of a grave. Jen-Jen jerked her hands up into the air as if rising out of one.

"I wouldn't understand," Todd repeated. He felt like a giant firecracker had gone off in his hand. His ears rang with it.

Before they could even sit down, Cha-Cha and Geno knocked on the door, yanking Angie forward while she pulled away from the light.

"We thought maybe it'd be better if the four of us tried to explain, you know," Geno said.

"Nah, Geno, I don't think so. I think that's the problem the kids are having—the four of us together," Bobbo said quickly.

Geno stood in the doorway, Angie still trying to pull herself free. Jen-Jen moved to stand beside him. "Geno might have a good idea," she said.

"Yeah, you guys taking your extra turns, you can talk all you want . . ." Bobbo said.

Angie screamed. Todd tried to slip out the door, but Geno blocked his way, then put his hand over Angie's mouth. She bit it and ran.

"Shit," Geno said, shaking his hand. He turned to look at Angie speeding off down the dirt trail that led up to the main road, a trail their parents had never been on.

"So much for getting our stories straight," Cha-Cha said. She looked at Bobbo as if expecting him to do something, but he had closed his eyes and lowered his head. If the four of them had been walls to a house of cards, his was folding, and the others would have to find a way to hold each other up.

Todd glanced carefully at each adult: no one was looking at him. "I'll catch her," he said, slipping out under Geno's arm and lunging out the door and into the woods on the thin trail behind Angie. No one chased after him.

"Angie," he shouted ahead. "Angie. They're letting us go," he said, but his breath stuttered with fear. "Angie," he shouted again, then he saw her turn and stop when she reached the main road.

He caught up to her, then, gasping for breath, he bent at the knees. He leaned his forehead into her shoulder.

"We have to . . . we have to think," he said.

"They don't care," she said. "They're just going to go back inside and fuck each other again. That's all they care about. Fucking."

Todd pulled at his own hair. "I bet they're getting in a car. Or sicking Carl on us. Maybe both." A single bulb shone its dirty light on the "Carl's Friendly" sign. Todd picked up a rock and whipped it at the bulb but missed hitting even the sign.

"They don't care," Angie repeated in a strange monotone.

"They care enough," he said, leading her into a ditch at the side of the road, on the edge of the thick woods. He felt like they were still in the boat, anchored. He fought against the feeling of surrender, of waiting to be found. He fought against the pull of his parents, who, he knew, did not hate him.

"I can't live with them," Angie said. "Never. I can't live with that."

"They seem all fucked up back there," Todd said. "It's like they don't even know who's who."

"Maybe they'll kill each other and let us be."

"They can't let us be, that's the thing. Can we trust anyone?" he asked.

"Well, not Carl," she sneered. "I want to call my grandmother."

"Is it against the law, what they've been doing? I never heard of people doing this—as a—as a kind of—"

"Goddamn hobby," she spat. "Like a fucking hobby. . . . Even if it was against the law, guess who's a fucking lawyer?"

Todd listened for any sign of tenderness in her voice. He needed that thin, sweet string to hold onto, but she was pulling all the strings back in. She was wrapping herself tight with them. Every time he thought of their parents in bed together, he felt his whole body spasm, revolt, reject the drug.

"But if word got out, wouldn't it ruin their careers? Their lives? They exposed us to it, and we, we're minors. . . . We have to live with this forever . . . whether it's public or private," he said. He kept trying to catch his breath, glancing up at the empty road, expecting to see headlights, to hear an engine winding up the hill from Carl's. The moon was already looking smaller, one side eroding, pulled back into night. "Forever," he repeated.

"Legally, we're runaways," she said. The closest pay phone was outside the IGA in town. "My grandma will believe us," she said. "If it doesn't give her a heart attack."

"They'll separate us," he said. "Like we did something wrong, not them. . . . I don't even have any change." He dug into his pockets. "No ID." He wondered how long she'd kept her suspicions to herself and why. He bent down to take her in his arms, but she stood and brushed off her jeans.

"I don't think I want to have sex, ever," she said. "Let's go."

"I don't think it's a crime," he said.

"What's a crime?" she asked.

"Go where?" he asked.

Their words were disconnected sounds scattering like stars loosed from their places. Whatever constellations they had imagined had fallen to earth in a shock of total darkness.

She stepped back up to the road and onto the yellow stripe down the middle of the two-lane blacktop toward town. He followed. He wanted to stop and hold her. She wanted to complete the marathon, but she wasn't sure he could keep up.

"I never want to see your parents again," she said. "Or mine."

"They're back there blaming each other. We can't blame each other. I don't want to lose—I'm not even sure I found you yet." He felt tears emerge and slide down his cheeks and onto his neck.

"Everything we did together was part of some kind of lie," she said. "They're *false*backs, not flashbacks. We can't trust any of those memories."

"But it wasn't our lie," he said. "Nobody can make somebody like—love—somebody else," he said. "You *know* that, Angie."

"We should have the only rowboat in the world," she said.

"A magic rowboat," he said.

"It doesn't have to be magic," she said. "It just has to be the only one. This isn't a game," she said. He felt like he was disappointing her. While she was pure white with crystal rage, he was simply overwhelmed. He just wanted to go back under the rowboat in the semi-dark and feel her warm, sweet breath again. "It's just not fair," he said lamely.

"That's why we have to leave," she said. She pulled her shirt down tight over her tiny breasts and tucked it in.

He felt like he'd been chosen to play a part in an action-adventure when he'd only signed on for a teenage romance. "Could I be anybody?" he asked.

She frowned severely. "What are you talking about?"

The mosquitoes were biting. He slapped at his own face. "This whole thing feels like it's on the wrong speed," he said finally, knowing it was just as lame. The week at Carl's had always been a time when every minute slowed down to be savored in the intimate boredom they shared, a sweet timeout from summer lessons, camps, chores, the monotony of their neighborhood streets, and the casual irritations of their friends. Todd felt like a huge section was missing. Just these two chunks of drama—he and Angie in love, their parents swapping—big boulders thrown against each other. Or two blown-up photos. He wanted to sharpen the focus on one and blur the other out entirely.

"You really don't have any money?" she asked. "Maybe if we go to the police, we'll get one phone call."

"Yeah, to our parents," he said. He didn't want to give in to hopelessness, but the new truth was slicing their past into bloody ribbons. "Maybe we could call Marina." He thought of her strong, broad shoulders, the burdens they could bear, had been bearing, but then he remembered what Carl had said.

Todd walked on the yellow line behind her, trying to catch her voice arcing back toward him. He reached into his pockets. A handkerchief. A pebble that he had planned to give her, green as her eyes. The kind of gift a child would give.

"Did we do something wrong? I feel like we did," she said, her voice softening. Her pace slowed, and he moved up beside her in the middle of the road. He took her hand, and she stopped and pulled it to her chest.

"How's my heart doing?" she asked.

He felt the quick, fluttering beat. He wanted to say something romantic and true.

"I'm so tired," she said. "Already." She didn't want an answer. She let go of his hand.

They heard a vehicle behind them, and together they turned. A pickup cruising slowly, scanning the sides of the road with the bright light poachers use for deer spotting. Angie stopped and Todd stopped. She took his hand again and held it.

They waited for the truck to find them standing right in the center of the road, not hiding at all. They waited to be caught in the headlights. To speak with the silence of deer.

ACKNOWLEDGMENTS

Cerise Press: "Held Back"
Exit 7: A Journal of Literature & Art: "Shocks and Struts"
The Paterson Literary Review: "Hurting a Fly"
Pig-in-a-Poke: "Threshold"
The Sycamore Review: "Candy Necklace"
Wake: Great Lakes Thought and Culture: "Scenic Outlooks"
West Branch: "Joyride"